OBSESSED WITH MY WIFE'S BEST FRIEND 4

A Novel by Lady Lissa & Shelli Marie

RECAP FROM BOOK 3

Tierra

Finding out that Tangi and Dallas had been sleeping around was one of the hardest things I've ever had to process. I mean, my best friend in the whole world had been carrying on with my husband behind my back. As much as I loved her, when I found that shit out, I felt pure hatred toward her. I had been confiding in her pertaining to my marriage the whole time she was sleeping with him. I felt like a complete fool. I guess that old saying about keeping your business with your man to yourself was true. I just didn't think that Tangi was capable of doing some foul shit like that to me. How could she call me her sister and fuck my husband behind my back? How could she fuck my husband behind my back and smile in my face?

Anyway, somehow, she and I found a way back to each other. When Thaddeus got shot by Dallas' crazy ass mama, I needed my best friend to be there for me. I couldn't imagine going through something like that without her. Who else could I call? I mean, of course, I called my mom, but Tangi had been there with me through everything. I needed her there and she was.

Thankfully, Thaddeus made a full recovery because I don't know what I would've done if he had died. He was everything that Dallas wasn't and then some. Even though Miracle wasn't his biological daughter, he treated her as if she was. He loved my baby more than I ever thought was possible and I was grateful for him. I couldn't have asked for a better man to help me raise my precious little girl.

I couldn't believe that Dallas was gone. Even though I had wished death on him, I never thought someone would actually kill him. I guess he had made more enemies than I thought. I wish I could say that I was sorry that he was gone, but to be honest, I wasn't. Dallas had made the last several months before he went missing hell for me. He was the one who had asked for a divorce, then when I finally decided to give it to him and move on he had a problem with it. He went borderline psycho on me.

When he went missing, I prayed that nothing bad had happened to him, but at the same time I was relieved to have some peace in my life. Finding out that someone had tied him up and dumped him in the bayou while he was still alive, that was a pretty cruel thing to do, but it is what it is. Dallas had done me so wrong when we were married and after we separated. I guess that was his karma.

Well, that's my story. Things couldn't be more perfect. But then again, maybe perfect wasn't the way I should describe it because usually when things are going too well, that's when something happens, and everything goes haywire.

Tangi

The fact that Tierra and I were able to make up and become besties again meant everything to me. I didn't care that it took a tragedy for us to get there. I was just glad that she was in my life again. I had really missed her. I had missed Miracle's cute little butt too. I'm glad that Tierra had allowed me to be her godmother and that she had agreed to be my baby's godmother. That's how it was supposed to be from the jump...at least before I had screwed everything up by messing with Dallas.

Trust me when I say, that was the worst decision I could've made in my entire life. I regretted that I ever slept with Dallas, especially because it could've cost me my friendship with Tierra. I should've known better and don't know why I allowed him to talk me into that affair. I couldn't believe how much Dallas was tripping on me when I decided to end the affair. Yes, he had left Tierra, but he had done it way too late. He should've left her when I was still interested in a relationship with him, but he didn't. He left her after he found out about my relationship with Smooth.

I don't think he ever planned on leaving Tierra in the first place; otherwise, he would've done it a long time ago. I think the only reason he finally left was to keep me from being with Smooth. That was his way of trying to control me, but it didn't work. When he came up missing, I wondered what happened to him, but I was happy. I didn't want him in my life, so when he was found in the bayou, I felt no sympathy for his ass. He deserved every bit of what happened to him.

I know that might seem harsh to say, but it's how I feel. I hated Dallas for what he put me through. By the time he was found, I had stopped caring about him a long time ago. The police still didn't know who killed him, but I wish I knew who did it. I would personally shake their hands and thank them because they really did me a huge favor.

What surprised me the most out of everything that happened was Ms. Armstrong's ass. I didn't know that lil woman had that much fuel burning inside of her. She was really tripping once she found out that Dallas was missing. I wanted to feel sorry when she died, but how could I? I mean, she was trying to kill my brother and my man. She got what she deserved, just like her foolish ass son.

I was so happy that Dallas was out of our lives. Now, I had my precious son and my amazing man. Not only that, but me and Tierra were besties again. The only thing that nagged at me was the fact that I was still holding on to this secret. There was no way that I could tell Smooth about the miscarriage that I intentionally caused. I hated keeping that secret from him, but I couldn't risk losing him again. He was my knight in shining armor. I know y'all probably think I'm a bitch for not telling him the truth, but put yourselves in my shoes. Would you tell your man that you took stuff to cause a miscarriage because you were pregnant for someone else when he thought the baby was his? I don't think so.

Naw, I said it before, and I'll say it again... this was one secret I'd take to my grave.

So, let's pick up where we left off, shall we?

CHAPTER ONE

Tierra

Two months later...

Thaddeus was finally beginning to heal physically from the gunshot wounds he suffered. Thank God! It could've been much worse, so I'm glad that he now had full mobility in his shoulder. We had postponed the wedding in Vegas because I needed to make sure my man was back to his old self before we got on that plane. He had gone back to work, but had been taking it easy and still needed to do so for the next sixty days. Either way, he was just glad to be able to get out of the house and back into the swing of things. With Thaddeus heavy on my mind, Miracle and I decided to stop by the gym on our way back from Tangi's place.

Without giving him a 'heads up' call, I headed over to surprise him with something that I knew was going to blow his socks off. However, when Miracle and I got to the gym, I didn't see him, so I went over to Hakim and asked where he was.

"Uh, he's in the office," he said nervously.

"Okay," I said and headed that way. But before I could take a good four steps, Hakim jumped in front of me.

"Um, he's kinda in a meeting right now. Maybe you should just talk to him when he gets home."

The fuck? Where did he get off telling me what I should do when it came to my man? Now, to be honest, on any other occasion I would've just agreed and left. But the nervous expression on Hakim's face had me thinking that whatever was going on in that office wasn't just an average meeting. He kept looking from the office door to me.

"Hey Miracle," he greeted my baby after several minutes of trying to hold me up. Yeah, something was definitely up with his ass.

"If I wanted to wait until I got home, I wouldn't have dropped by," I said smiling with a smirk.

Once again, I stepped around Hakim and started to head in the direction of the office. And once again, Hakim stopped me. "Look Tierra, this is our place of business. I don't mean any disrespect, but I don't need you making a scene up in here."

"Why would I make a scene in here? I just dropped by on my way home, so me and the baby could see Thaddeus. When have you ever known me to cause a scene when I come over here?" I asked.

Something was off and didn't seem right with his attitude, but I couldn't put my finger on it. If he didn't want me to make a scene, all he had to do was get the hell out of my way so I could go see my damn man. What the hell was so wrong about that?

"You're right. I'm just saying that he's in a meeting, so now isn't the best time to go into the office."

"You're silly. Why would I just walk into his office when I know he's in a meeting? That doesn't make any sense to me. Does it make sense to you?" I asked.

"Not really..."

"Right. I was going to sit and wait for him to come out of the office, if that's alright with you," I said as I continued to stare at him. Sure enough, his eyes became shifty and I could see his lips twitching.

"Okay. I just don't know how long he'll be," he said.

"Well, lucky for him, I've got all afternoon," I said as I flashed him a fake smile.

As it turned out, I didn't even have to wait because shortly after that, Thaddeus' office door opened and he, some chick with red hair and a little boy walked out. I looked at the unfamiliar female, who seemed to have an attitude, and then at my fiancé, who seemed to be just as nervous as his brother was when he saw me.

"I will be in touch Thaddeus. Hopefully, by that time, you'll be ready to do the right thing," the woman said as she patted him on the chest.

Humph. What the hell was going on between the two of them? Who the hell was that woman and what did she mean by do the right thing? As she passed me by while holding the little boy's hand, she kind of smirked at me. Shit, I didn't know who she was, but I was definitely curious as to why the hell she was smirking at me like that.

Thaddeus approached me with a nervous grin on his face and kissed my cheek. He took Miracle from me and held her close. "Hey babe, I didn't know you were dropping by," he said.

"Well, that's obvious. Who was that woman?" I asked.

"Nobody important," he said.

"Well, what did she mean by you doing the right thing? The right thing about what?"

"Can we talk about this when I get home? I really have a lot of work to do since I've been so backed up," he said downplaying the situation.

"Yea, sure. We can talk about it when you get home, but don't think this is going away. We promised each other no secrets," I reminded him.

"I know."

I took the baby from him and left without saying anything else. That shit was too suspicious and if that woman would've been outside when I stepped out, I would've approached her and asked her what was going on. That was some shady shit.

Seeing her nowhere in sight as I approached my car, I unlocked the door and placed Miracle in her car seat. I sat behind the wheel feeling very heated. I wasn't the jealous type by any means, nor was I insecure. That was just some suspicious shit that any woman would've raised her eyebrows to. I mean, put yourself in my shoes before y'all say I'm overreacting.

I show up at my man's place of business to visit with him for a few. Immediately after arriving, I peep game on how nervous his brother is. Then he blocks me not once, but twice from heading that way. Then when the door finally opens, here comes my man, some strange woman and her kid. Then she has the nerve to pat him on the chest and tell him that she'll be in touch and hopefully he does the right thing?

That would make any woman suspicious about what was going on between them. If Thaddeus thought that I was going to forget about that little exchange by the time he came home, he could forget about it. As I merged onto the highway, I pulled out my phone and called Tangi. I needed her to tell me that I wasn't overreacting even though I knew that I wasn't.

"Hey girl, are you calling to give me all the juicy details?" Tangi asked when she answered.

"Nope. I didn't even get a chance to tell him," I said. Shit, I had totally forgotten the real reason I went to see Thaddeus in the first place.

"What? Why not?"

"Girl, I got there, and Hakim stopped me from going into the office."

"Why did he do that?" she asked.

"He fed me some bullshit about how Thaddeus was in a meeting. If he wouldn't have been so nervous and jumpy, I probably would've just left and texted Thaddeus to let him know I came by. But Hakim was way too jumpy, and he blocked me like twice."

"Well damn! Sounds like he was trying to keep you from finding out something," she said.

"Good! I'm glad you said that because for a while I thought I was trippin'!"

"Heck naw, you weren't trippin'! Something was clearly going on that they didn't want you to know about!"

I breathed a sigh of relief because I was glad we were on the same page. If she had told me that I overreacted, I probably wouldn't have said anything to Thaddeus about it. But since she said what I thought, yea, I was going to say something to him.

"So, did you ever find out what they were hiding?"

"Not really," I explained letting her know about the chick that came out with him.

"That doesn't mean anything. She could've been a client," Tangi reasoned.

"Tangi, I might have believed that if she hadn't patted him on the chest and said she would be in touch and hoped he'd do the right thing," I huffed with irritation.

"Wait, wait, wait! She touched his chest?"

"Yes! That's exactly what she did!"

"So, what's the right thing?"

"Shit, I don't know! He said we'd discuss it when he came home," I explained.

"Oh, hell yea! We would definitely have to discuss that shit when he came home! What kind of shit was that?" she asked.

"Tangi I don't know what the hell is going on, but you can best believe when he comes home, I'm gonna find out!"

"Tierra calm down. You might be getting pissed about nothing. He might have a reasonable explanation for that," she said.

"I'm trying to calm down Tangi, but everything about that situation smells funny!"

"The two of you are getting married in a couple of months. Please don't let something that might be innocent have you feeling insecure..."

"Insecure?! I'm not insecure, even though I should be after what you and Dallas had put me through, but I'm not gonna go there!"

"Good, because I've apologized more than enough, and you said you forgave me."

"Of course, I forgave you Tangi, but I didn't forget!"

I hope she didn't think I had forgotten that shit. I wished I could forget, but unfortunately, I couldn't. This conversation was going all the way left and pissing me the hell off even more than I already was. The nerve of her to call me insecure. If I was insecure in any way, it was because she and Dallas made me that way! But this shit with Thaddeus had nothing to do with my insecurities.

Something about that wasn't right and I was going to get to the bottom of it!!

CHAPTER TWO

Thaddeus

Now shit was about to hit the fucking fan! Right when I get my life together and make something of myself, here comes Sheena! The first chick I ever loved and first chick to break my heart.

When Hakim came and pulled me from a training session, and his eyes were bucked, I should've known something was up. The last thing I expected was to see Sheena standing there with a kid that she was claiming to be mine at that! Then, if that wasn't already bad, Tierra shows up with Miracle to surprise me while I had Sheena all closed up in my office! Imagine that shit! Talk about bad fucking timing, man! I had to do something before I talked to my fiancée.

"Man, what the hell was that all about bro?" Hakim asked drawing me right back into my office once I got both Tierra and Sheena to leave.

"Close that door behind you."

After my brother shut it and turned around, I began to explain to him how Sheena had just shown up and claimed that I was the father of the child she had with her. "So, let me make sure I got this shit straight, bro. Sheena ran off with that baller from out in west Texas. She's been with him for the past four years and now that they've broken up, she comes up here to see you and all of a sudden, that little boy is yours?"

"Yeah, that's basically what's happening bruh. I didn't even wanna tell Tierra no shit like that until I found out if the lil' boy is mine or not, but now look at this shit! I ain't got no choice but to tell her at this point. I mean, I'd hate for her to find that shit out from someone other than me!"

"Have you even told her that you still got your own place?" Hakim pressed with a raised brow as he stood there staring down at me.

"She knows I haven't sold it yet..."

"But does she know that your things aren't packed up and you still go there..."

"That is my space when I need some time alone..."

"You have a whole office here and we are open 24 hours..."

"Why are you trippin' bro?!"

"You are unnecessarily keeping secrets that could possibly ruin your relationship with Tierra and if you love her like you say you do... you need to come clean before shit blows up in your face."

"That's not gonna happen because I'm gonna do this DNA testing bullshit and prove that little boy ain't mine!"

"How do you know he ain't yours?" Hakim questioned calmly with a twisted lip. "Now that I'm thinking about it, that little boy looks like he's about four or five. She could've been knocked up before she left here."

"Why would she wait until now to tell me then bro?" I pressed in need of a clear understanding.

"Because that nigga left her ass and now, she needs somebody to help her raise her son." Hakim enlightened like he had all the damn answers. He just thought everything was so fucking simple. "Either that, or you really are the baby's daddy."

"No fucking way nigga! I can't be! Not now!"

"Why not now?!" Hakim asked with a smirk.

"Because I'm in love with Tierra and I'm about to marry her."

"Oh, so where is it written that you can't have a son and marry Tierra too?" he clowned waiting for an answer.

"Shit, I don't know what's what right now, but I need to find out and standing here talking to you about it ain't gonna get that shit done," I huffed as I gathered my keys and cell to leave. "I gotta get the ball rolling on the testing shit so that I can move forward with my life. I really don't wanna fuck up what I built with Tierra over something that I didn't even know about."

Checking the clock, I saw that it was nearly noon. That gave me six hours at tops to deal with Sheena. Then I would have to deal with Tierra.

"Let me shoot her this address and have her meet me there." I thought out loud as I drove my car from the parking lot of the fitness center and headed to my house that was located fifteen minutes away.

My modest three-bedroom, two-bath home was nothing compared to the 3,500 square foot estate I shared with Tierra. She had expensive taste and had it all decked out while my place had modern furniture and décor. Truthfully, I had ordered most of that shit online while I sat at home bored.

"It ain't much, but it's mine!" I sighed heavily as I walked through the front door and kicked my shoes off.

Immediately noticing the foul odor seeping from my armpits, I flew through the shower and changed into some more gym clothes. By the time I got out and slid into my new sneakers, the doorbell was chiming.

Taking my time to answer it, I stepped slowly to the door before swinging it open. There I found Sheena dressed in that same tight ass red dress that matched her hair. Her titties were damn near popping out the top! I tried not to look because I was a taken man, but damn!

"Hey, come on in," I said breaking the awkward moment.

Gesturing Sheena to come inside and into the living room, I asked her where her son was. "He goes to camp in the afternoon. I don't pick him up until four."

"Good, that gives us time to talk about getting this paternity test done. I need to know now..."

"Why... was that your wife that came up to the gym earlier today?" Sheena asked while entering my personal space.

Backing up, I took a seat on the recliner and answered her. "She's not my wife yet. She is my fiancée and..."

"And your daughter?"

"Yes, my daughter."

The more I looked into Sheena's eyes, the more the feelings from the past began to stir inside me. The shit was making me confused. I mean yeah, of course, I was deeply in love with Tierra and loved Miracle like she was my own, but Sheena did something to me. It was like she had this power of seduction over me. She was so much different than Tierra. She was a confident hood chick that knew how to use what she had to get what she wanted. Therefore, I had to remind myself to tread lightly with her ass.

"Is that your only child besides our son, Dillon?" Sheena asked shaking me from my daze.

"Speaking of which, when can we take that paternity test? Let's call and schedule it now." I suggested as I took my cell out and Googled a list of nearby clinics that had quick results.

After finding one a few minutes later, I dialed them to make the appointment for 4:30 that afternoon. Right after Sheena had to pick him up from camp.

"That gives us two hours to catch up." Sheena purred as she batted her eyes and crossed her legs displaying her thick thighs.

"Okay, let's go to the diner down the street." I suggested while picking up my keys to throw her a hint.

Catching it right off, Sheena sprung to her feet and beat me to the door. "Let's take separate cars. I'll meet you there."

Meeting up the street at Armando's, I got Sheena and I a table by the window. She arrived just as I sat down.

"Hey, I wanna thank you for not tripping on me when I just showed up at your gym unannounced."

"My gym?" I asked to see how much she knew.

"Yeah, now you're gonna act like you and Hakim don't own the chain of…"

"We own a couple of franchises," I said cutting her off. "I'm engaged, I'm in love and I'm happy."

"Congrats. I just want you to know that the last thing I'm here to do is cause problems."

"Well then why the hell would you wait until now to show up?" I asked becoming a little on edge about the whole thing.

"I told you because by the time I found out that I was pregnant, I had already moved with Duper to Midland," she explained. "By that time, it just didn't make sense to involve you. I mean, we both had moved on so..."

The whole line of questioning seemed pointless. I wasn't going to get any of the answers I wanted, so the only thing left to do was to get the answer I needed from the paternity test.

Wrapping up our late lunch, we left the diner. I went back up to the gym and took care of a few things while Sheena went to pick her son up from camp.

An hour later, I showed up at the clinic fifteen minutes early. I sat in my truck and waited for her to arrive. When she didn't arrive five minutes after the designated time we were supposed to take the test, I called her and called her and called again. Shit, I called for the next twenty minutes with no response. What kind of shit was that? Like we just saw each other a little while ago, and she said she'd meet me after she picked up her little boy. Why the hell wasn't she here and why wasn't she answering the phone?

I continued to try and reach her for twenty more minutes, still without any response. Finally, I just gave up and headed home. I didn't know what the hell I was gonna tell Tierra about Sheena's ass. I had hoped that I could at least tell her that I had taken a paternity test and would have the results for her in a few days, but I couldn't even tell her that.

I couldn't believe how my life had suddenly been turned upside down this way. This morning, I woke up feeling on top of the world. I kissed my woman and baby before I left for work. I never thought this was how I'd be ending my day. Shit, I couldn't even say that if Sheena had disappeared, I could forget about her ass because I couldn't. What if that little boy was mine? That meant I'd have a kid running around somewhere without his father in his life.

It wasn't the child's fault that his mother and I weren't together anymore. I owed it to that little boy to find out if he was mine... but gotdammit, where was his fucking mother and why hadn't she shown up to the lab?

Leaving there by 4:30, I rushed home to talk to Tierra about everything that was going on, but right when I got there and was ready to spill the damn beans, Tangi called her. It must've been an emergency because Tierra tore up out of there like a leaf in the wild wind while I was left there all alone to tend to Miracle.

I guess I don't have to worry about having that discussion about Sheena and her son tonight...

With a deep sigh of relief, I fed Miracle, gave her a bath and put her to sleep. Shortly after I placed her in her crib, I dozed off too...

CHAPTER THREE

Tangi

When Tierra hung up on me, it instantly hit me that it was probably because I was being a rude ass bitch. I mean, she was calling to talk to me about her man problems and I was trying to get her to see things from another perspective. The thing was, my baby boy had been extremely fussy with a cold for the past few days.

He had been coughing, sneezing and running fever... not to mention congested like crazy. The only thing that would quiet him down was if I put the vaporizer on. That would calm the congestion, but he would still be wheezing which really had me worried. Usually Smooth was here to help me with him, but right now he was down at the club working as usual.

"What could be wrong with you baby? I've been giving you medicine!" I cried as I walked around bouncing my 10-week old son in my arms as I paced back and forth in my bedroom.

I was contemplating taking him to the hospital because he wasn't eating. He had spit up the little milk that he did drink earlier. I was just so tired.

My eyes were swollen not only from crying, but because I had barely gotten any sleep. Between the sleepless days and nights from the baby hollering, I couldn't get a moment of peace unless Smooth was around. I had taken my baby to the doctor a couple of days ago and she said he only had a little cold. I couldn't even understand how he had gotten a cold in the first place. He was just so young. His symptoms seemed to be getting worse, especially his breathing, which had me deeply concerned.

"That's it!" I hollered out in tears as I watched my son gasp for air while coughing.

Gathering his things and stuffing them in the diaper bag, I got Samuel and rushed to the hospital once again. On the way there, I touched the dashboard screen and dialed Smooth to tell him where I was going to be. When he didn't answer the first or second time, I was forced to send a text.

"Fuck!" I yelled over Samuel's cries. As long as he was screaming, he was breathing and that was keeping me calm enough to drive. "Please, please God! Don't let nothing seriously be wrong with my baby!"

Dialing Tierra, I got her on the line right away. I could tell that I was interrupting something, but I needed her. I only prayed she would be able to come because at that point, I had no one. My mom had decided to take a cruise, so she was going to be gone for the next four days. Since Smooth wasn't answering, who else was going to be there for me if I didn't call Tierra? No one, that's who.

I pulled into the hospital parking lot fifteen minutes later and drove around to the emergency room entrance. After parking my car, I rushed to get my baby and practically ran through the double doors of the hospital.

Dashing up to the desk, I breathlessly started speaking. "My baby is having trouble breathing and he feels like he's running a fever!" I said as I struggled to catch my own breath.

She quickly jumped into action, taking the baby from my arms and rushing through the double doors that led to the emergency area.

"I NEED HELP! I HAVE A BABY IN DISTRESS!!" she cried.

The nurses and a couple of doctors quickly rushed over and took Samuel from her. After placing him in a small hospital bed, the doctor had a worried expression on his face.

"HE'S NOT BREATHING!!" he called out.

Next thing you know, I was being ushered out of the room. "No, I'm not going anywhere!" I insisted trying to remain in the room with my son.

"Ma'am you have to let the doctors do their jobs. I promise that your baby is in good hands!" the nurse assured.

"I'M NOT LEAVING!!" I demanded through pursed lips. I watched with tears flowing from my eyes as they performed CPR on my little baby.

"Ma'am please. Is there someone I can call for you?" she asked.

That's when I remembered that Tierra was supposed to be meeting me. I decided to head back out there to see if she was here yet. As soon as I made it back to the waiting room, she was walking in. I walked straight into her arms and just started bawling. She held me tight as I cried on her shoulder.

"What's wrong? Is Sammy okay?" she asked.

I just shook my head and kept crying. After several minutes, a nurse walked over to me. "Excuse me ma'am, I need to ask you some questions so we can get your baby registered," she said.

I was trembling so badly because I didn't know what was going on with my son back there. I could only pray that they were able to save him.

"I need to find out how my baby is," I sniffled feeling distraught.

"I'll see if I can get some information for you," she replied nicely as I followed her to her area.

Once she got me seated, she began asking me questions about my baby concerning his eating habits and his breathing. She wanted to know if he was having trouble eating or anything specific that I might have noticed about him recently.

"Well, aside from the breathing issues and fever, he hasn't been eating that much either."

"When was the last time he's seen the doctor?"

"A couple of days ago."

"Let me see if I can get the doctor to come speak with you," she said.

"He'd better come speak to me because when I left the room, my baby wasn't... he wasn't..." As tears began to rain down my face again, I felt a terrible aching in my heart. I rocked back and forth in the chair as Tierra held my hand.

"Let me see what I can find out," the nurse responded before hurrying off.

"Tierra what if my baby died?" I asked as I cried.

"He's not dead Tangi."

"What if he is? I don't know what I'm gonna do without my baby!" I began to cry uncontrollably at that point.

The thought of losing my son caused the biggest pain that I've ever felt. I didn't even feel that pain when I lost the first baby, but now. Oh God! Was this God's way of punishing me for getting rid of my firstborn? Was this my karma for everything that I had done wrong to Tierra?

In the midst of my worrying, the nurse returned with a doctor. I jumped out of the chair, anxious to hear what he had to say.

"How's my baby? Please tell me he's still alive!" I begged.

"Your baby is alive..." the doctor said.

"Thank God!" Tierra said.

"Can I see him?" I asked.

"Well, Miss Carter, I need to have a conversation with you first."

"About what? You said my baby was fine! Please... I just need to see my little boy!" I cried.

"I promise that I will take you to him as soon as we're done talking," the doctor guaranteed.

"Why do you have such a serious look on your face?" I asked.

"Well, first of all, I need to properly introduce myself. I'm Dr. Lance and I'm one of the pediatricians here at the hospital..."

"Please, just tell me what's wrong with my baby!"

"Well, Miss Carter, your son has pneumonia," he said.

"PNEUMONIA?!!" I shrieked.

How could such a little baby have pneumonia? How could my baby have pneumonia when I took him to the doctor a couple of days ago? Why didn't the doctor tell me that my baby was so sick?

"Yes ma'am."

"Hold up! I just took my baby to Dr. Jackson the other day. If he had pneumonia, why didn't she say something?" I asked.

"I'm not sure why the doctor didn't tell you. It could be because it hadn't developed into pneumonia at that time. Did the doctor tell you that he had a cold?" Dr. Lance asked.

"Yea, and that's all she said!"

"And that may be the only thing that was wrong with him at the time. But if he wasn't prescribed the proper medication that would be why his condition worsened instead of gotten better," he stated.

"Is he going to be okay?" I asked as the water works began to flow again.

"Well, when you brought the baby in, he was unresponsive for a short time. However, we managed to get him breathing again and he's stabilized. However, we are going to have to admit him into the Neonatal Intensive Care Unit so we can monitor him for the next few days," Dr. Lance said.

"Oh my God! So, my baby has to be in ICU?"

"Yes ma'am."

"Can I see him? Please!" I begged.

"Give us a few more minutes to make sure everything has been properly connected..."

"What do you mean?"

"We have your son on several monitors for his breathing. He's also on oxygen to help him breathe properly," Dr. Lance said.

This was too much. My baby was only a few weeks old. He wasn't old enough to be dealing with all this shit. He was still a newborn.

"Is my baby gonna die?" I asked nervously.

"As I said, your baby is stabilized at this time. We're going to continue monitoring him for the next few days. Do you have any more questions?"

"I just wanna see my baby," I cried.

"We'll come and get you when he can have visitors. Don't worry Miss Carter, we are taking very good care of your little boy."

That's easier said than done.

As my worried thoughts consumed me and the doctor walked away, I collapsed in Tierra's arms again. I hope she knew how grateful I was that she was there. I don't know what I would've done if she hadn't been.

Ring, buzz, ring, buzz... My phone began to ring, so I pulled it from my pocket to see who was calling.

It was Smooth. I picked up the phone, but didn't say shit. I was pissed that he was just calling me now, almost two hours later.

"Tangi? Are you there?" he asked.

"You're finally calling me? I left you voicemails and text messages and it took you almost two hours to return them?"

"Well, I am at work. We were busy?"

"Yea, I bet you were busy!" I said sarcastically.

"What's that supposed to mean?"

"It means you need to get your ass down to Texas Children's Hospital ASAP!" I said before ending the call. I didn't have shit else to say to his ass.

Hell, our son could've died tonight, and he was just getting back to me now. That was unacceptable!

CHAPTER FOUR

Smooth

Tangi was blowing up my phone from the afternoon until the evening, but I couldn't respond because we were busy. Once shit had calmed down, I finally hit her up. I was expecting her to be upset because I ignored her calls, but I wasn't expecting her to say my son was in the hospital. I mean, I knew he had a slight cold, but to be taken to the hospital again?!

Yeah, I knew that it had to be that serious when Tangi hung the phone up on my ass. Without trying to dial her right back, I rushed over to Jay to let him know what was going on. He was going to have to lock up without me because I needed to go check on my son.

"Aye bro, I gotta head out," I said nervously.

"What's going on with you? Everything alright?" he asked, concern on his face.

"Nah, Tangi just called and asked me to meet her at Texas Children's. That means something is wrong with Sammy. I gotta go check on that," I stated.

"Yea, yea. Go ahead. Hit me up when you know something or if y'all need anything."

"Thanks bro." We gave each other a brotherly hug and I was outta there.

The whole half hour drive it took me to get to the hospital, I tried calling Tangi back, but she wouldn't answer. I needed to know what was going on with my boy. I already felt bad enough that I couldn't answer when she called all those times because we were hosting a televised event at the club. Shit, Tangi didn't even give me a chance to explain that shit and now she wasn't even answering back. That right there was just spiteful and petty. I was gonna have to check her ass about that shit when I got there.

Childish ass shit!

Fussing silently as I pulled into the parking lot not knowing which way to head, I veered right and snatched a spot near the emergency room then rushed inside. Right when I entered the hospital and hit the corner, I found both Tangi and Tierra pacing the floor in the waiting room.

"What's going on?" I asked, worried about Sammy.

Tangi stopped pacing and glared at me. "Oh, so you finally decided to show up, huh?"

"Tangi I'm sorry, but we were busy at the club..."

WHAP!

"You said that me and your son would always come first. I don't wanna hear shit about that damn club!" she barked as she pointed her finger in my face with tears streaming down her flushed cheeks.

Tierra stepped in between us to try to diffuse the situation that had already gotten way out of control. I just wanted to know what was going on with my son! Not get whacked in the fucking face!

Ignoring Tangi's rant, I turned to Tierra hoping that she would be a bit more level-headed than my soon to be wife. "Can you please tell me what's wrong with my son?" I asked as I directed my question to Tierra.

Tangi huffed loudly and rolled her eyes at me before walking out of the room while shaking her head.

"Don't mind her. She's just upset by the news."

"What news? What's wrong with my son?"

"Well, Tangi brought him in here because he was having trouble with his breathing. By the time the doctors got to him, he wasn't breathing at all..."

"Are you telling me that my son is..." I immediately felt a strong tug against my heart. That shit was hurting like I was about to have a heart attack, but I knew it was just because of what my woman was going through. Man, if my son had died and I wasn't here for her...

As tears slowly seeped from my eyes, Tierra quickly said, "No! No! The doctors were able to save him..."

"Oh, thank God!" I said as I started crying. "Where is he? I need to see him!"

"He's being admitted into the Neonatal ICU. He has pneumonia..." she said.

"PNEUMONIA?!"

"Yea, that's why Tangi's on edge. Pneumonia is very serious in babies, especially newborns like Sammy. It can have a major effect on his physical and mental..."

"What the hell?!" I gasped feeling fucked up inside for not being here when she first called.

"Go be with them. I'm gonna go call Jay for Tangi and let him know what's going on. I'm sure he's gonna wanna be here," Tierra said patting me on the back before walking away.

Going to find Tangi, I went to the nurses' station to ask for some information. Luckily, the woman working behind the desk came and escorted me to the back where they were just about to transfer Sammy.

Easing beside Tangi, I interlaced my fingers with hers, and we walked over together. "I'm sorry," I whispered while gripping her palm tightly.

"You're here now and that's all that matters," she assured with a forced grin and tears streaming. "Sammy needs the both of us."

"And that he's gonna have," I promised as we entered a secured area.

Stopping us at the first desk, the nurse had us fill out some documents while the doctors got our son situated.

"Is this all? Can we see our son now?" I pressed growing impatient. "They have all those tubes shoved up his tiny little nose and..."

"Stop! You're making me more nervous than I already am Sam!" Tangi fussed breaking down in loud cries. Her high- pitched screams sent chills over me.

I knew that she was going through it because she never called me Sam. A couple of months ago, she started feeling the name out, I guess. Lately, she had been calling me by my government name quite a bit. I thought it might be because of Sammy's name, but now I was starting to think it was because she would just be aggravated with me.

"Ma'am, do you need the doctor to come out..."

"No! Y'all better not sedate me or no shit like that! I wanna be awake because my baby needs me, and I need to know what's going on with my son!" Tangi screamed over and over until they finally came out with the syringe and knocked her ass out with a heavy dose of something before sliding her onto a gurney and taking her off to a room. I was glad they did too because she was not only making a scene, she was working my damn nerves!

"I'm sorry..." the nurse from behind the desk said with a shrug.

"Don't be. Now maybe I can get some answers," I told her with a laugh.

Coming around from the side, the nurse handed me some scrubs with head and feet coverings then escorted me to where Sammy was. Slipping into everything then washing my hands, I eased on the face mask and followed the nurse into the room.

"Hey lil man, it's daddy. You sure know how to get your mommy and daddy's attention...not that you didn't have it already. You okay buddy?" I whispered as I neared the clear crib they had him in. Sammy's eyes were closed, and he had tubes everywhere and an I.V. connected to his little arm. He looked way smaller than his little 12 pounds.

As I stood there and watched his tiny chest heave up and down, my heart went out to him. I felt like shit for not getting here sooner. My son was lying in a freaking hospital bed with pneumonia while I had my ass up in that damn club. I should've been here sooner. I should've responded when Tangi kept calling. Watching my son's little chest go up and down was fucking crushing my soul.

"Is he in any pain?" I asked the doctor that was on the other side of the crib checking Sammy's vitals.

"No, he's comfortably resting right now."

"What can be some side effects of all this at such a young age?"

"Honestly, this hit Samuel pretty hard. Hopefully, we caught the pneumonia early enough so it doesn't leave any lasting effects on him. With him being so young, I'm gonna have to keep him here for a few days. We'll be able to determine the long-term effects once he's breathing better. Sometimes, kids his age have to use a small oxygen tank..."

"What?!" I asked in shock as I swallowed hard.

"Yes, I'm afraid so."

"What about long-term effects?"

"Let's not get ahead of ourselves. I'll just give you some informational pamphlets so that you can read up on your son's condition. If you have any questions or concerns after that, our staff is here 24 hours to assist you," he said before nodding and leaving the room.

Coming back moments later as I held onto my son's hand, the doctor returned with several booklets. After thanking him, I sat in the chair and began reading them, but didn't get to the second page because by then, Tangi came rushing in. She was trying to talk, but I couldn't understand shit she was saying with the face mask on.

"What?"

"There can only be one in at a time," the nurse repeated giving me the signal to let Tangi stay.

Not wanting to make a fuss, I left out and stripped out of my scrubs then went back to the waiting room. Surprisingly, Tierra was still there and now, Jay was with her. They seemed to be in a deep conversation until I approached then and cleared my throat.

"Oh, shit!" Jay said jumping to his feet to pound his fist with mine. "What's up with ya shorty? He cool?"

As I filled him in, Tierra stood there and listened. Neither of them could believe how serious shit had gotten or how fast.

"Damn, I'm here if you need me man," Jay sighed before sitting back down. "The club is cool, and we don't have another event for a couple of weeks."

"Aight, I just hope Sammy makes a full recovery from this shit."

"Did they say he might not?" Tierra gasped with tears in her eyes.

I began to explain about the information the doctor gave me to read. While I was showing the material to Jay, Tierra got a call. When she got off, she seemed irritated. She stated that Thaddeus was on the phone and she needed to get back home.

"Yo, go handle yo shit at home and I'll call you and keep you updated on Sammy's condition," Jay told Tierra as he hugged her.

Saying goodbye to us both, she walked out the double doors. When she disappeared, I looked at Jay. His eyes were glued in her direction.

All I could think was... *What the hell is this nigga thinking?*

CHAPTER FIVE

Tierra

"Damn!" I giggled as I slid into my ride and headed home from the hospital.

I should've been ashamed of myself feeling all giddy when I should've been worried about Sammy. It was all Jay's fault too!

Sure, Tangi's brother had always flirted with me since we were young, but either he had a girlfriend at the time or I had a husband, so shit didn't ever work out. Now, here he was at it again and I was engaged to Thaddeus! Ugh!

I couldn't even lie though. The attention Jay's fine ass was giving me made me feel alive again. I hadn't felt that way since before I was pregnant.

Sure, Thaddeus paid me compliments, but they were more routine than anything. He just hadn't been the same since he got shot. I honestly thought he was low-key blaming the whole thing on me when he knew what he was getting into when we started this damn relationship. Now this fool was being sneaky about some shit. Yeah, I was on my way home to find out just what the hell was going on.

Arriving at the house a half hour later, I walked in boldly ready to question Thaddeus about the chick from earlier. I was so glad to find him still wide awake and Miracle fast asleep in the nursery.

"So, how's Tangi's son?"

"He has pneumonia, so they had to admit him. He's in ICU," I briefly explained.

"Pneumonia? ICU? Damn! Her baby is so young," he said.

Yea, yea, yea! That nigga thought making small talk about my godson was going to get him off the hook with that shit at the gym earlier. Hell naw!

I just ignored his false concern and got right to the point instead. There was no beating around the bush. "So, you wanna tell me about earlier at the gym?"

"Well, ah, yeah..." he started stuttering and shit. That told me that it was about to be some mess.

With my stomach in knots, Thaddeus poorly enlightened me about some ex-girlfriend named Sheena that he never mentioned before. When he paused, I waited for more because the story he was giving me was damn sure incomplete. Some shit was missing, and I needed answers.

"So, why is she showing up now? Is there something she needed?"

"Well, ah, yeah..."

"Well, what was it?!" I pressed not understanding why the bitch was at my fiancé's job sweating him after not seeing him for years! Touching all on his chest and shit. No, something was going on.

"She's trying to say that the little boy she had with her..." he paused and swallowed hard before returning his gaze back to me. "She's saying the kid is mine..."

That was all I heard before I lost my voice and my damn mind because I threw the first thing that I got my hands on at him; the lamp, then the remote, then a shoe. That nigga got to ducking and dodging everything I slung his way.

"Why the fuck you ain't tell me that it was a possibility that you could have a child roaming around some damn where?!" I shouted. "What else are you hiding from me Thaddeus?!"

"Why are you trippin' like this Tierra?! I said I didn't know shit about this until Sheena showed up at the gym today..."

"But you ain't never even mentioned no Sheena to me ever before and now out the blue you have a son?!" I cried realizing that I had been betrayed yet again. That shit hurt. "You know what?!" I shouted angrily before snatching my keys and purse. "I'm leaving! You stay here and look after Miracle since you in the daddy mode nigga!"

Slamming the door behind me, I drove straight over to Jay's club. There I knew I could get as drunk as I wanted to, and he would make sure that I would get home safely.

Please don't let this fool start flirting and shit. I'm gonna need him to be in a brotherly mood and give me some sisterly advice on how to deal with Thaddeus and his 'maybe' baby mama.

Parking my car in the lot of the club thirty minutes later, I entered and went straight to the bar and ordered a double shot of Hennessey. After downing that first one, I slammed the glass upside down and ordered another one.

"Damn, shit didn't go so well at the home front huh?" Jay clowned as he walked up from behind me and sat down on the stool next to me.

"Nope!" I said as I knocked the second drink back.

"Damn! You wanna talk about it?"

"Not really," I said as I looked at the bartender. "Gimme another one!"

"Damn girl!" Jay said in shock. "I ain't never seen you drink that much so fast..."

"That nigga might have a child..."

"What the hell? And he ain't said shit to you?"

"Hell no! He's claiming that he didn't know nothing about the kid either. Like how could he not know?" I asked as I chugged another one back. By this time, my head was a little woozy from the three shots I had consumed.

"Wow! That's some crazy shit," Jay said.

"Shady shit is more like it, but I don't even wanna think about that right now. I just want to drink my problems away and deal with everything else tomorrow. Am I so wrong for feeling that way?" I asked staring Jay directly in his slanted brown eyes. I never really noticed how much he and Tangi looked alike until just now.

"Maybe he didn't know. I mean, that shit is possible these days. Bitches get pregnant all the time and either hide the shit, blame it on another nigga or really don't know who the baby daddy is. Real shit Tierra," Jay smirked and stood up holding his hand out.

"What?" I asked not quite understanding.

"Let's go sit in the VIP area so we can talk in a more secluded setting."

"Oh, you gonna give yo lil' sis some advice?" I giggled as I stood up and realized that I was already fucked up. My legs were a little wobbly as I tried to gain my composure. The last thing I wanted was to look like some wino in this club and in front of Jay.

Quickly wrapping his arm around my waist, he allowed me to lean against him. *Damn! Why did he have to smell so fucking good?*

"Yeah, and I'm gonna give you some support to make sure you don't fall on your way over there!"

Jay was clowning, but was the perfect gentleman the whole evening. He even ordered me all kinds of food to make sure I didn't get sick from all the alcohol I was consuming.

"You straight?" he asked as he checked the time on his cell. "It's almost closing time and that nigga is gonna come looking for you if you're not home soon."

"Let him come look for me!" I slurred still giggling as I rose from the bench, stumbled forward and landed against Jay's chest. "Mmmmm, you smell fucking delicious!"

"See, now yo ass is trippin'. Let me take you home."

"Oh, you taking me to my house or yours because you know I ain't never seen your crib before. You wanna show me?" I pressed with an uncontrollable laugh.

"Stop playing and get your purse. I'm gonna get you an Uber or take you home."

"Well take me home then, but not my house," I said giving him a flirtatious gaze with a wink. I knew I had no business trying to wade in that water, but my feelings were hurt, and my pussy was throbbing. It just needed a little attention. I wasn't going to fuck him. Just play a bit.

I mean, it wasn't as if Jay was a stranger to me. Shit, we had been knowing each other since we were kids. *What's wrong with a little forbidden foreplay between friends?*

"You need to stop Tierra because when a nigga did try to holla at you, yo ass didn't wanna give me no play. Now you got a man, not to mention a baby girl, you wanna kick it with a nigga?" he teased as he headed for the door and escorted me outside. "Never mind. Don't even answer that. Give me your keys." Digging down in my purse, I handed the remote start controller to Jay who in turn handed it to the security guard that was standing near us. "Follow us down the street so I can get this girl home."

"Gotcha boss."

We all walked out into the parking lot... well, they walked, I stumbled. The cool breeze was the only thing that stopped me from closing my eyes. Straining to keep them open, I got in the passenger's side of Jay's SUV and tilted the seat back. Then it was over. All I remembered was hearing the music playing and Jay talking over it.

"I can't take you home like this. That man is gonna shit if he sees you like this." I heard him mumbling to himself.

Good!

As far as I was concerned, he didn't need to take me home. I didn't feel like going home right now anyway. What I did feel like doing was having some fun with Jay's fine, smell good ass. I didn't bother responding to anything he was saying as I got really comfortable in the seat of the expensive truck.

Remembering things only in flashes, I felt Jay park the car. He helped me inside an unfamiliar dwelling and laid me on something soft. My head was spinning, and my stomach was turning. Then there was silence.

An unknown amount of time went by and I found myself sweating. To get a little relief, I peeled out of my clothes down to my bra and panties and tossed and turned for a while until I dozed off...

It wasn't until the sun rose and beamed through the window that I realized I wasn't home. I must've sprung up like a Jack in the box, but it was too late, Jay was standing there in the doorway staring down at me with my half-naked ass.

Hell yeah, I was embarrassed, but what could a bitch do?

CHAPTER SIX

Thaddeus

I was glad that I told Tierra about Sheena and what was going on, but I didn't get to tell her about me keeping my house. When she asked if there was anything else that I was hiding, I should've just come out and told her, but instead, I lied once again. I mean, she was already pissed so it didn't make sense to piss her off even more than she already was.

After all that arguing about it, Tierra wound up leaving mad and I went to bed. I figured once she had a little time to cool off, we'd be able to talk things through. Hopefully, by morning she'd be in a better position to hear me out.

Only when I woke up, she still wasn't home. Staying out all night was something that she had never done before, so I wasn't sure how to take it. I mean, was she at a hotel? Did she go back to the hospital to be with Tangi? Where the hell was she?

Not wanting to assume the worse, I called her phone after I changed and fed Miracle. As I listened to the phone ring, I bounced my baby girl in my arms and watched as her eyes slowly closed.

"Where is your mommy and why isn't she answering her phone?" I whispered as I gently laid the sleeping baby in her crib. I left the room and continued to dial Tierra over and over again until I heard the front door close and the alarm beep.

Greeting her at the steps, I began my interrogation. "So, you were at the hospital with Tangi and the baby all night?"

"No," she answered nonchalantly as she brushed by me and went to the bathroom to start the shower.

That shit sent up a red flag. "Why the hell you coming straight home and jumping in the shower, huh? Why you gotta wash yo ass first? You should be talking to me first?"

"Did you talk to me first when, ah, what's her name.... oh, yeah, Sheena! Did you talk to me first when Sheena came up to the gym?"

"You're acting childish as hell about this shit Tierra!"

"Worry about getting that paternity test then get at me Thaddeus. Until then, this unsettling feeling that I have in my stomach is not gonna go away."

"So, that's it?"

"No! It won't be it until you take the damn test! What's the hold up?" she snapped nastily.

Ain't that a bitch! Here she was standing there like she hadn't done shit wrong! She had stayed out all night and came home smelling like liquor and cologne, but was still on me about a fucking DNA test! Aw, hell nah!

"I'm gonna get the test as soon as possible baby, but what I don't need you doing is reacting by doing something stupid. You know once you do some disrespectful shit, you can't take it back?!"

"Like you getting that Sheena chick pregnant?" she questioned sarcastically with her slick ass tongue before slamming the bathroom door in my face.

I wanted to kick that muthafucka in, but my cell started ringing and distracted me. Especially when I saw it was Sheena calling. Yeah, she had a whole bunch of explaining to do behind that little disappearing act she pulled.

Taking advantage of the time I had while Tierra was taking a shower, I went out back to take the call. "Hello?"

"Before you start trippin' Thaddeus, give me a chance to explain."

"Explain?"

"Yes, explain. Look, when I went to pick up our son from camp, he was itching like crazy. I lifted his shirt and found out that he had broken out in fucking hives! So, I had to take him to the clinic and get some injections. He won't be feeling well for a few days, so we're gonna have to put the testing off for at least a week," she explained.

Now, as inconvenient and coincidental as that was, what the hell could I do about it? I mean, damn. Like just yesterday the kid was fine, but now, he's gonna be down for a week. I wondered was she even being honest with me or if she was stalling.

"A week?" I asked. "So, what you're telling me is that my life is gonna be on hold for at least a week?"

"I know it's an inconvenience, but it's not my fault. I didn't plan for that shit to happen. I didn't expect you to be trying to deny our son either. I mean, he looks just like you."

Okay, now she was reaching because that little boy looked nothing like me. Women liked to say that shit even though they knew that it wasn't true. She's telling me that kid looks like me, but when the DNA test comes back negative, who will he look like then?

"He does not look like me..."

"Yes, he does! You can deny it all you want to, but when that test comes back positive, you'll see it then!" she argued.

"Whatever! If that little boy was mine, why didn't you tell me about him sooner?" I asked.

"Because we had both moved on..."

"I don't give a shit! That doesn't give you the right to hide a child from me if he's mine! I should've been told as soon as you found out and the fact that you hid it from until he was four or five..."

"He's four!"

"Well, FOUR years old is ridiculous! That's one of the main issues I have with believing your story. Look, hit me up when you're ready to do the test. Otherwise, I have nothing else to say," I informed her.

"Are you serious?"

"Damn right I'm serious! I haven't seen you in almost five years Sheena. Then all of a sudden out of the blue, you whisk back into my life and expect me to play daddy to some kid I never knew about! That's some foul shit and I ain't with that!"

"I'm sorry for keeping our son..."

"YOOOOOOUR SON!!" I interjected. "Ain't no way I'm finna take the heat for being that kid's pappy without a test."

No way was I going to allow her to push this kid on me just because she didn't know who the real daddy was.

"Wooooow! You really doing it like that, huh?"

"What you thought that I was just gonna accept what you said and start dishing out money? Nah!" I huffed.

"Umm umm!" I heard Tierra clear her throat from behind me.

Rolling my eyes as I ran my hand down my face, I turned around to come eye to eye with her. Right off, I knew she wasn't happy with the way shit was going, but that wasn't my fault. I didn't ask Sheena to show up here and fuck my life up. She did that shit on her own.

"Look, the bottom line is we need a DNA test before I accept any responsibility for that kid. So, whenever he feels better, let me know and I'll RESCHEDULE that appointment," I insisted while clinching my cell tightly.

I emphasized the word 'reschedule' so that Tierra would know that we did in fact have an appointment previously. I needed her to know that I wanted to know if that kid was mine just as much as she did.

"Damn Thaddeus! It's like that?" Sheena blurted out loudly.

"Like I said, let me know when your son is doing better so we can get this shit over with!" I repeated before ending the call and sliding my cell into the front pocket of my gym shorts.

I gave Tierra a smirk that should've said, "I told you so". Instead of giving me props for being honest, she twisted her lip and threw her hand in the air before walking back in the house. I followed behind her because I wasn't trying to keep arguing with her. I loved this woman, so we needed to fix this shit right now.

"You couldn't wait to call your baby mama huh?" she asked with an attitude.

"First of all, she called me and secondly, of course I'm gonna speak to her because I need to get that DNA test done ASAP because you been trippin'!"

"I've been trippin'! Men always say shit like that when they fuck up!"

"I didn't fuck up! I told you that I knew nothing about that little boy until yesterday! But we not gonna keep going on and on about that when yo ass was missing all last night. Where were you Tierra?" I asked as I crossed my arms over my chest.

"Why do you need to know that?"

"The fact that you even asking me that question makes me nervous. I mean, you came in here after being out all night long reeking of alcohol and men's cologne..."

"What?" she asked as she laughed nervously.

"You know it's true. I just wanna know where you were last night. That's the same question you'd be asking me if the shoe were on the other foot!"

"I was just out, alright?"

"Oh, so that's what we doing now?"

"What do you mean?" she asked.

"We're engaged but can stay out all night now?"

"No!"

"Then what? Where were you and I'm not gonna ask you again," I said.

"Don't talk to me like that! You ain't my daddy!" she barked angrily.

I didn't know what was happening, but I needed to get out of there before I said something I'd regret. She stayed out all night but had the nerve to be angry with me. She didn't deserve that right. She should've brought her ass home last night instead of rubbing against whatever nigga she was all up on. I walked to the bedroom and grabbed my wallet. I put it in my pocket, put my shoes on and headed back to the front room.

Grabbing my keys off the hook in the kitchen, I went through the door that led to the garage. Tierra ran up behind me as I opened the door to my truck.

"Where are you going?" she asked.

"Where were you last night?" I asked again.

"I already told you that I was out!"

"Well, I'm going out!"

I slid into the driver's seat and opened the garage door. "So, we playing tit for tat now? Don't you think that's a bit childish?"

"Call it what you want! Right about now, I don't give a fuck!" I said angrily.

Backing my truck out of the garage as she stood there glaring at me, I shook my head. I knew that she was mad, but I didn't care. She had no right to be that mad behind some shit that was out of my damn control. If I could've prevented Sheena from bringing her ass around here, I would have... and still, that didn't give Tierra a free pass to act the fucking fool.

We were engaged to be married in a couple of months. We would've been married by now if I hadn't gotten shot because of the shit going on between her and her deceased mother-in-law. Shit, what would she have done if we would've been married right now? Go out and fuck with some man because she was pissed? That wasn't about to fly with me.

I knew the only one who would understand me was my brother. So, I headed over to the gym to get his advice because the way things were going now, Tierra and I were definitely headed for *Splitsville*.

CHAPTER SEVEN

Tangi

Two days later...

Things between Smooth and I had definitely not been good. I tried to let the fact that he wasn't here for me sooner go, but I couldn't. I was deeply troubled that he chose to ignore my calls instead of checking to see why I had been calling so much. I mean, if I couldn't count on him in the case of an emergency, what the hell did I need him for? That right there showed me that he wasn't ready for the same thing I was ready for. Maybe I needed to rethink marrying Smooth even if we had a son.

"You okay?" he asked as he rubbed my shoulders.

The doctors had finally cleared it so we could both be in the NICU at the same time. I mean, we both were worried about our son, so it didn't make sense for both of us to have to switch up every so often. It made more sense for both of us to be in the room, especially if Sammy's condition took a turn for the worst. The doctors were confident that he would make a full recovery, so I remained hopeful.

"I'm fine!" I said with an attitude trying my best to stay angry with him.

Exhaling deeply, Smooth sat in the chair next to me. "Look Tangi, I know this is a stressful time for you, but it's also stressful for me. That's my son in that bed too," he said through clenched teeth while trying to keep his tone low.

I turned to look at him and rolled my eyes. I decided that I wasn't going to fuss with him, not here, not now. Our son was still very sick, so he needed both of us to be here. For his sake, I wasn't going to keep going at it with his father.

"Let's not argue," I suggested taking the conversation a different direction until the nurse came in to check Sammy's vitals. She marked everything in the tablet that she held.

"How's he doing?" I asked.

"He's doing better. The medication we're giving him is keeping his temperature from spiking up. He's still wheezing and congested, so we're gonna give him a breathing treatment today. Don't worry Miss Carter. Your son is in very good hands here. We have some of the best doctors taking care of him," she assured with a smile.

"Thank you."

"You're welcome."

She walked out of the room leaving me alone with Smooth once again. "Do you wanna talk about this shit? I don't want to keep arguing with you Tangi. I love you. I love our son. I want this to work," he said.

"This isn't the time or the place. We can talk about this later..."

"Later when? We don't know when Sammy is going to be released from here. Shouldn't we try to clear the air now, so there won't be so much tension when we all get home?"

"Look Smooth, if you feel there's too much tension in here for you to be here, feel free to leave. You won't force me to discuss shit that I ain't ready to talk about. I just want to focus on our son and be there for him. Everything else can wait!" I snapped trying not to get riled up again. I wasn't about to be playing with them damn doctors about sedating me. That shit wasn't cool.

"Ugh, yo ass is straight trippin'!" he mumbled under his breath.

I gave him that look that said I was done talking. I don't know why he couldn't see that this wasn't the right time to discuss our personal issues. I didn't care what he wanted to discuss right now because the only thing that mattered right now was getting my son home.

"Alright," he said and stood up. He walked over to Sammy and kissed him on the forehead. "I'll be back."

"Where are you going?"

"I just need some air."

"Yea, okay."

"Yea, I'm out!" he said and left without so much as a kiss on the cheek.

I was glad he hadn't tried to kiss me though because I definitely would've put my hand up. The last thing I wanted was for him to be trying to kiss me after everything that had been going on. As far as I was concerned, he could stay gone until we got back home...

Just as I got settled in the recliner next to Sammy's crib and took myself a nap, Smooth came back in the door apologizing. No matter how mad I tried to be with him, I couldn't. I was too damn tired, mentally and physically.

"Look, go home and get yourself cleaned up. I'll stay here with Sammy," he offered.

"It's okay. I'll stay..."

"No, you've been holding this shit down ever since he was admitted. It's my turn now. Go home baby, jump in the shower and change into some fresh clothes. You will see what a difference the simple shit can make," he insisted with a kiss to my forehead. That shit always got me.

"Are you sure?" I pressed double checking his offer.

"I'm positive, now go."

Heaving myself from the recliner, I went over and kissed Sammy before departing the room.

"Hey Tangi," Smooth called out right as I was fixing to walk out.

"Yea," I said and turned to face him.

"Take your time. I'll be here and ain't going nowhere," he said. That shit right just melted any animosity that I was feeling toward him a few moments ago. He was such a good dad, which made me believe I had overreacted before.

I knew that Sammy was in great hands, but that didn't stop me from feeling guilty for leaving my son as soon as I reached the parking lot.

"Maybe I should go back?" I debated out loud as I got inside my car and turned the key in the ignition. Then I looked down at my clothes. Shit, I was a hot mess.

Instantly deciding to hurry home and get back to the hospital as fast as I could, I peeled out of the parking lot and hopped on the main road. As I hit the next left, I thought about Tierra.

Just to touch basis with her and put her up to speed on what was going on with Sammy, I auto dialed her on the dash screen. "Hey sweetie! How's Sammy?" she sang through the speakers loudly.

Turning down the volume using the feature on the steering wheel, I hit the next corner and headed north. "He's holding up."

As we began to chat, I quickly briefed her on Sammy's condition. Then came her turn to talk.

"So, me and Thaddeus have been going at it, girl!"

"Huh?"

Tierra told me all about what was going on in her household. I wasn't a bit shocked until she said she stayed out all night.

"What? Where the hell was yo lil' fast ass at all night long?" I teased giggling like a teenager.

"With my friend..."

"Yo friend who?" I pressed dying to find out who it was.

"My friend..."

"A male friend or a female friend?" I laughed.

"Does it make a difference if it's strictly platonic?" Tierra laughed.

"No, but my nosy ass wanna know anyway!" I replied playfully.

"Forget all that and get yo ass home so you can get back up to the hospital to be with Sammy. I sure hope he gets better soon. Matter of fact, call me when you get back up there so I can have an excuse to leave tonight."

"You sneaky lil' bitch you!" I teased. "Even though I'm the last person that should be saying a thing about this, but... please be careful boo. If you really love Thaddeus..."

"I do love him, but these secrets and all this betrayal shit got my head and my heart all messed up. It's not just that Thaddeus may have a son. It's the fact that he lied to me about it even being a possibility. Not only that Tangi... I know he still cares about that Sheena chick. Just by the way he looked at her that first day and the way he gets defensive when I even bring the shit up. You know men do that shit all the time. Soon as you bust them in a lie or doing some mess that they had no business doing, they flip it and get mad at the female! Like we did some shit! Ugh, I swear!"

"Well, are you in love with him Tierra or do you think you fell for him as a rebound?" I asked making her evaluate her feelings. She paused for a few seconds before answering.

"Thaddeus was there at the right time and said and did all the right things and everything was going great. He loves Miracle and I love him for that, but ever since he got shot, things haven't been the same between us. It's like he changed... shit, we've changed. I can't explain it," Tierra confessed sadly.

"Awww, I'm so sorry boo. I didn't know that things weren't good at home. I didn't know it was that serious."

"It wasn't until this shit with Sheena popped out the fucking closet!" she fussed. "I think that was what really pushed me to the limit and now that nigga mad at me!"

"Don't trip Tierra," I urged as I pulled up in my driveway and went inside my house. "Things always have a way of working themselves out. If you and Thaddeus really love each other and want to be together, I truly hope y'all can get it together. I just want you to get the happiness that you deserve."

"Yeah, well, we'll see," she sang out.

"Keep the faith Tierra," I told her. "I'm at home now and I'm about to run in here and take a quick shower then change. I'll call you soon as I get back to the hospital so you can come down and we can talk some more because you gotta tell me who this 'friend' is girl!"

"Hush heffa and make sure you call me!" Tierra giggled then hung up before I could speak another word.

That girl is crazy!

Laughing to myself as I rushed through the shower and changed, I thought about Smooth and how our relationship had taken a turn for the worse as well. We too were going through a rough patch.

While I'm over here giving Tierra advice, shit, I need to get my own house in order!

As I drove back up to the hospital an hour later, I thought about the health of my son and the shaky bond I had with Smooth. I needed him to get on the same page as I was if things were going to work. I just prayed that he wanted a family just as bad as I did. If not, I was going to have to do shit on my own. Either way, I knew that I was going to be good...

CHAPTER EIGHT

Smooth

After I just stormed out on Tangi like that, I realized that I wasn't just walking out on her. I was walking out on Sammy as well and that wasn't sitting good with me. That's why I went back and stayed with him while she went home to get cleaned up.

Soon as she left, Sammy was out and then I fell asleep right behind him. I didn't wake up until Tangi came in and shook my shoulder. She said that she had already been there for a couple of hours. Shit, I had slept the whole damn day away.

"Babe, I just talked to the doctor," she whispered. "He said Sammy can go home in the morning, but he has to be on a breathing machine. They have to train us to use it…"

"How long does he have to stay on that shit?" I asked, stretching and yawning as I stood up and let Tangi have the recliner.

"I don't know and the last thing I want to do is sit down. I'm so anxious and worried that I don't know what to do with myself," she admitted with tears beginning to trickle down her face.

Taking her into my arms, I let her know that everything would be alright even though deep down inside I knew that it was a good chance that things would only get worse. With Sammy needing oxygen 24/7 and the odds for him having a full recovery being slim, I had no idea what the future held for him. All we could do was love him through it all without driving each other crazy.

Honestly, I hated that Tangi and I hadn't been getting along since she had the baby. Blaming it on postpartum depression was easy for me, but now I saw that it was much more than that. She was seriously tripping. One minute she hated me and the next she loved me. I just didn't get it.

"Smooth, are you listening to me? The doctor is about to come in and show us how to use the machine while the nurse takes Sammy down for some more tests," Tangi repeated becoming irritated with me.

Before I could shoot some slick shit back at her, a couple of nurses came in to train us on the use and care of Sammy's breathing machine. The tall white nurse began sorting everything out on the side table as the short skinny one began to get my son ready to go.

"The testing will take about an hour or so. Please feel free to go and get some fresh air or something to eat after the fifteen minute training session," the shorter nurse suggested before taking Sammy away.

Tangi and I looked at each other and smirked then turned to the taller nurse. She caught on really quick and turned that fifteen minute session into a five minute one.

"This machine should be pretty easy to use, but I hate my son has to..."

"Our son?!" I snapped tired of her trying to be sarcastic.

Just as the argument was about to break out, Tangi rushed off to the attached bathroom crying. I just stood there shaking my head.

"I don't mean to pry," the taller nurse whispered after creeping in the room without me seeing her. "I just wanted to say that this could be a stressful time for parents. I mean, having your newborn hospitalized has got to be hectic, but you both have to be there for each other. Your wife seems to be taking things really hard. Just try to be there for her. She's going to need you to have more patience with her and more understanding. I know it's going to be hard at times, but it will bring you closer after all is said and done."

"Thank you. I'm starting to think she's suffering from postpartum. She hasn't been the same since the baby was born," I offered.

"Well, she'll need to see a doctor to get a diagnosis for that."

"How long can that last?" I inquired.

"Well, I've been in this field a long time and I see this much too often; families falling apart because they can't take the stress from a baby's illness."

"How long?" I pressed starting to feel bad about snapping on Tangi so hard.

"Sometimes months, but the less stress, the quicker it will pass." She smiled before leaving. "I will have the doctor discuss this in further details."

As the door swung shut behind the nurse, I went to the bathroom, and apologized to Tangi. She was still full of tears.

"I'm so sorry, but I don't know what's wrong with me! One minute I'm okay and the next I'm crying and sad, then the next I'm angry at the world!" she sobbed loudly.

Shushing her up with kisses to her lips, Tangi embraced me and held on for dear life. It was like she needed me, and my heart went out for her.

"Baby it's gonna be alright," I promised not knowing what the future held. "I'm here..."

"For how long though?" she cried looking up at me. "If I were you, I would've left me a long time ago! Look at me! I'm a mess! I've done so much wrong that maybe this is God's way of saying that I don't deserve you! I don't deserve the perfect family and the Lord is showing me by letting this happen to Sammy! It's my fault..."

Even though a lot of what Tangi was saying was true, I couldn't stand to see her like that. I had to comfort her.

"Come on baby. Pull yourself together. We have another half hour before they bring Sammy back. Let's go outside and get some fresh air and..."

Cutting me completely off, Tangi drew me even closer and began kissing me while unbuckling the belt that held my jeans up. Soon as they dropped to the white tiled flooring, I knew what was up; my manhood.

As Tangi stroked it into the perfect erection, she slid her dress up and her pink lace panties to the side. Allowing me full access to her vanilla scented stash, I pinned her up against the wall before beginning to penetrate her at a slow pace.

"Oh, yes!" she moaned while digging her fingertips on my lower back.

Throwing that ass right back at me to match my stroke, Tangi let me know she was climaxing. I could tell because her pussy began to drip. That shit turned me the fuck on even more. That and the fact that we were having sex in the damn hospital bathroom was what made a nigga bust in a matter of seconds. The shit felt so damn good that I didn't want to take my dick out of her. I just stood there holding her body up against the cold wall.

"I'm sorry," she whispered looking up at me. "I love you so much."

"I love you too." I replied as I finally released her and wet some paper towels for us to clean ourselves up.

Taking a deep sigh, I smiled as we exited the room hand in hand to take a walk outside. Since that sex session only lasted two minutes, we still had that half hour left.

Making small talk as we took the elevator downstairs then walked outside in the cold darkness, we began discussing Sammy's future. It was all good until she didn't agree with me on something.

"Why do you always have to go against me?" Tangi fussed.

"Here you go…" I mumbled under my breath as we stood out in front of the hospital under the light.

"Yeah…"

"Hey y'all!" Tierra screamed out as she approached us from behind. "I know it's late, but I promised that I would come and check on you guys and Sammy."

The two hugged and now they were both smiling. As long as it kept Tangi's nasty mouth shut it was all good by me.

"Okay, I'm gonna go inside..."

"Wait, hold up!" Jay yelled out coming up from behind in the same direction that Tierra had just come from. "I was just coming up there to check on you guys."

"Oh, so both of you just happen to come up here, at the same time, huh? And after visiting hours at that?" Tangi probed sneakily while I stood there waiting for the answers because I knew something was odd about the shit.

"See, now yo ass is trippin' sis!" Jay insisted as he dapped me up and gave both Tangi and Tierra a quick hug. Well, he gave Tangi a quick one. Tierra's lasted a little longer. Yea, I peeped that shit.

"No and let me find out that this is the friend that..." Tangi blurted out before Tierra elbowed her in the side.

"Come on and let's go check on Sammy!" Tierra insisted dragging Tangi back inside the hospital.

Once they disappeared, I gave Jay the eye. "Nigga what's up?"

"Not this cold ass weather that's fa sure. Let's go inside."

As we entered into the lobby of the hospital, I looked around to make sure Tangi and Tierra were out of earshot. Then I hit my boy with some questions.

"So, nigga what's up with you and ol' girl?" I pressed.

"Who? Tierra?" he shrugged and laughed. "That's my sister's home girl and I've known her since we were kids..."

"Yea, I know all that shit! I ain't talkin' about that!" I said as I eyed him suspiciously.

"Then what are you talking about playa?"

"You know exactly what I'm talkin' bout!"

"Nigga I'm confused as fuck right now. If you wanna know something, just ask."

"Are you and Tierra fucking around?"

"Well damn! What would make you ask me some shit like that?" he asked.

"Humph! The fact that you keep answering my question with a question tells me everything I need to know," I said.

"Well smart ass, in answer to your 'question', nah. It ain't nothing like that. I used to feel strong for her back in the day, but she was always too bougie and shit," Jay said with a chuckle.

Nah, something was definitely going on between them... no matter what he said. I had been knowing him for way too long, and I knew that every time he chuckled like that, he was hiding something.

"And now?" I clowned. "The way you lookin' at her man, I can tell you wanna fuck with that." The expression on his face spoke volumes once again. "Shit or maybe you hit it already!"

Jay didn't answer me that night, but he really didn't have to. His facial expressions told it all...

CHAPTER NINE

Tierra

I was really messing with Tangi's head when I was hinting around to having a new friend. She would trip if she found out that it was her brother I was talking about!

Right as the thought crossed my mind, Jay called to check on me. The conversation was short and there was absolutely no flirting whatsoever. He just asked if I was okay and I told him yes, and he said he would talk to me soon. That was it!

Truthfully, after that I wasn't even considering hooking up with Jay's fine ass again until Thaddeus came home drunk an hour later and passed out. Can you believe that shit? He had been gone all fucking day and when he finally came back home, his ass was ta-ka-la!!

I decided that was a good time for me to go through his phone and find out what he was up to while he was away. Yeah, maybe I shouldn't have gone through it, but I was glad I did. Because if I hadn't, I would have never seen all the text messages between him and that Sheena bitch. They were flirting back and forth about the old days and shit.

As the anger rose within my body, I walked over to the bed and hovered over him with my fist balled up. It took everything in me not to wake him up from his drunken slumber with a right punch to the jaw. I wasn't crazy though. I just waited until he woke up that night and sobered up enough for me to leave Miracle there with him. I got dressed while he sat in the living room watching ESPN. Soon as I walked by him, he jumped up.

"Where are you going?" he asked in a huff.

"Out!"

"Oh, hell nah!" Thaddeus yelled. "You ain't finna run yo' ass up outta here again and try to stay out all night! This shit ain't gonna keep happening Tierra."

"Lower your voice before you wake Miracle up!" I hissed and rolled my eyes. "I'm going to the hospital to give Tangi a break! Yo' ass over there worrying about the wrong shit!"

"The hospital huh? Yea right!"

"I'm telling the truth and if you don't believe me that's probably because you have some shit to hide!" I countered. "That's your own guilty conscious talking!"

"Don't put that shit on me! I'm not gonna be putting up with that shit every night!"

"Nobody asked you to! My best friend's son is in the hospital, so I need to go check on him and be there for her!" I said.

He looked at his watch then back at me. "You need to go be there for her at almost nine o'clock at night? You do realize that visiting hours are over now right?" he asked.

"So? I don't need it to be visiting hours for me to go up there. She's my best friend and I'm Sammy's godmother!"

"Tierra you don't need to go over there right now! If that's where you're really going," he mumbled.

"I heard that slick shit! That's your insecurities talking," I said.

"Insecure?! You think I'm being insecure?"

"Well, aren't you? Trying to stop me from going visit my friend and checking on my godson..."

"IT'S ALMOST 9:00!! That shit can wait until morning!" he hissed.

"I don't wanna wait until morning," I said as I grabbed my keys and purse.

"Tierra you better not walk out that door..."

"See you when I get back!"

Flipping my hair over my shoulders without a care in the world, I flew out the door and headed to the hospital. I knew that visiting hours were over, but I didn't care about that. I just wanted to get out of there. No, I needed to get out of the house.

On the way there, Jay called to check up on me again. *Hmm, twice in one day huh?* A bitch was feeling really lucky and my ego was soaring right about now. I always had a crush on Jay since I was a kid. How could I not crush on him? He was tall, chocolate and very appealing... just like my favorite Hershey's candy bar. What I liked most about the man that Jay had become was how protective he was of the people he loved. That turned me on more than anything else. I loved a man who took care of his family.

"So, it sounds like you're out in traffic already," Jay probed.

"Yeah, I'm actually on my way up to the hospital to check on your sister and nephew."

"Oh yeah? That's where I was headed."

"Well, I guess I'll see you in a few minutes then," I giggled. "Why don't you meet me in the south parking lot?"

"I'll be there in ten."

Well, I was a lot closer than I thought, so I made it there in five. I would've waited for him, but when I saw Tangi and Smooth out in front arguing, I had to go over there and find out what was going on.

So much for trying to keep shit on the low. Even though there was nothing going on between me and Jay, I was standing there looking dumb as soon as he joined us all outside.

Shit, he gave me that enticing stare that had my damn panties getting wet! Then when he hugged me! The way he held me and stroked my back, with his fresh minty breath against my earlobe; the intoxicating scent of his cologne damn near made me cream in my panties, but Tangi's ass had to try to clown. I shut that shit down real quick and dragged her ass inside.

"Don't be making a fool out of me like that?" I hissed playfully as we got in the elevator to go to the private waiting room they had upstairs near where Sammy was.

"So, Jay is the secret friend you were talking about, huh bitch?!" Tangi hollered and hugged me. "You two are some sneaky muthafuckas!"

"It's not like that!" I insisted while low-key lusting over that nigga.

"Then what is it like?"

"I don't know. What I do know is that I have feelings for your brother and they just came from out of nowhere..."

"What about Thaddeus?" Tangi asked.

"I don't know. We haven't been getting along since he was shot and all. I mean, he blames me for what happened. Then this Sheena bitch came around with all that baby mama drama. It's just been too much for me to deal with. Jay, on the other hand, has been very supportive and easy to talk to."

"So, what does that mean?"

"I don't know. I think I might ask Thaddeus to move out..."

"What? Did you and Jay have sex or something?" she asked in a hushed tone. I didn't answer right away, so she started talking again. "Ouuu y'all nasty!"

"It's not like that!"

"Then what's it like bitch? Talk to me! You know I'm here for you and I'll never betray your confidence," she said.

"I know, but it's not something I wanna discuss right now. I need to figure out how to tell Thaddeus that I think it's best for us to live apart for a while."

"What the hell are you saying Tierra?" Tangi gasped.

"I'm saying that I need some time and space to make some major decisions. Plus, if that little boy is Thaddeus' son and I find out he's been hiding that or anything else, I'm done. I'm tired of being betrayed by the ones I love..."

"I know boo, including me. I can't apologize enough for what I put you through." Tangi sniffled as the tears began flowing. "It's all my fault! Everyone's life spiraled out of control because of my selfish actions..."

"You didn't act alone, and I forgave you for all that. My heart and head are just so messed up behind it and all I want to do right now is take care of Miracle and enjoy life... stress free! I mean, Dallas ain't around anymore and my life is still fucked up!" I said sadly.

"It'll get better Tierra. God has something special in store for you. Dallas wasn't good for you and maybe Thaddeus isn't the right one for you either. Maybe my brother was who you were supposed to be with all this time. Wouldn't that be something? My best friend and my brother linking up for their happily ever after."

"Wait a minute now bestie," I said. "I'm still in a relationship with Thaddeus. I can't even think about me and Jay in that way right now!"

"But you like him. I know you do. I'm just letting you know that I approve."

"Well, thank you for your approval, but right now it's a little premature."

"So, when are you going to talk to Thaddeus?" Tangi asked.

"As soon as I get home."

My phone beeped signaling a text message. I pulled it from my pocket and saw that I had a message from Jay. I guess my smile was bigger than I thought it was because Tangi crossed her arms and stared at me with a huge smile on her face.

"What?" I asked.

"That must be my brother," she hinted.

"Would you please stop?"

"Okay. Well, I'm gonna go check on Sammy. He was taken downstairs for tests and may be coming home tomorrow if they all come back okay," she said.

"That's great sis! I hope the tests prove to be positive."

"Me too. Now, you go on and text my brother back. I'm just gonna go see if Sammy's back in the room."

I didn't confirm or deny that it was Jay on the phone. She walked away and I opened the text to see what he said.

Jay: R u still w/Tangi?

Me: She went to check on the baby

Jay: Wyd

Me: Waiting on her

Jay: How long u gon' b waiting?

Me: Idk... why?

Jay: Come meet me

I giggled when I saw that. I didn't know why he had me so giddy. I felt like a fuckin' teenager right now.

Me: Way

Jay: Same place I was waiting for u earlier

Me: Gimme 15

Jay: Aight

I tucked the phone back in my pocket and paced the floor while waiting for Tangi to return. I thought about sitting in one of the cold hard seats, but I couldn't stay still long enough for that. A couple of minutes later, Tangi returned.

"How's Sammy?" I asked.

"They just brought him back to the room. I'd invite you to see him, but it's past visiting hours."

"It's okay. I'll come back tomorrow to check on you guys."

"Thanks Tierra. I don't know what I would do without you," she said as she gave me a tight hug.

"Well, lucky for you, you don't have that to worry about." I said with a smile as we released each other. "I'll call you in the morning."

"Are you on your way home?"

"Yea. I'm gonna go have that conversation with Thaddeus. I mean, ain't no time like the present," I lied.

I had every intention on speaking with Thaddeus concerning our relationship, but tonight wasn't going to be that night. As Tangi headed back to ICU, I headed to meet Jay. I ran into Smooth as he stepped off the elevator.

"You heading out?" he asked.

"Yea, Sammy just got back from the testing, so I'm gonna head home," I said.

"Okay, well drive safely."

"Thanks. Take care of my girl and godson," I sang out.

"You already know," he assured with a smile. Smooth looked exhausted, but I guess caring for a sick baby would do that to you.

As I hopped on the elevator and hit the button that would take me to the first floor, my phone started ringing. I figured it was Jay checking to see where I was, but when I checked the caller ID, I saw that it was Thaddeus. A quick jolt of guilt ran down my spine, but I ignored it. Our relationship right now was filled with uncertainty and chaos. I was in such high spirits right that minute that I didn't want him to bring my mood down. I turned the ringer off right as the elevator dinged and stopped on the first floor.

Once I exited, I couldn't wait to get to Jay. It was like my feet were trying to run when my body was trying to walk. I'm telling you... my insides had some strange shit going on.

As soon as I rounded the corner, I spotted Jay standing against his truck with a huge smile on his face. My heartbeat became a little more erratic, almost feeling as if it was going to jump out of my chest. I couldn't get over there fast enough...

CHAPTER TEN

Jay

I had no idea what was going on between me and Tierra. I had been knowing this woman almost my whole life. She and I had several 'almost' moments, but never had the chance to go all the way with it. She was either involved or I was involved or we both were involved. I respected her and the relationships that she was in... until the other night.

I had taken her to my crib instead of hers because she was drunk. I didn't want to take her home that way when she had a baby to tend to. Since her dude was there for the baby, I took her to my place. The gesture was totally innocent on my part.

I didn't have any thoughts in my head about her and I or anything like that. I just considered myself helping out a friend. However, I wasn't expecting to get out of the shower and check on her to find her laying there in her bra and panties. The vision immediately sent my dick springing to life. I was absolutely stumped when I saw her. Seriously. My mouth was hung wide open. My dick was hard as a rock and I knew my damn face had lost all color.

I wanted to look away because I knew she was involved with the dude from the gym. But even though my mind was telling me no, my body was speaking louder when it screamed yes. As the two of us walked closer to one another, one thing led to another and we found ourselves butt ass naked on the sofa getting it in. Even though Tierra had given birth a few months ago, her body was still fit and tight.

My hands roamed over her plump butt cheeks as she rode and bounced up and down on my dick. She moaned as I kissed her deeply. I had never kissed Tierra before, so once our lips met I didn't wanna stop kissing her. Her lips were so damn soft.

Before we parted that morning, we promised each other that we'd forget about what happened and never bring it up again. However, once she left, even though I tried my best to stop thinking about what we had done, I couldn't. I couldn't get the visions of her plump ass out of my head. My lips still seared from the kisses we shared. I definitely enjoyed that night with Tierra. I knew that she was with that dude and I had every intention on respecting her relationship once again, but that wasn't how things worked out.

I found myself texting her constantly over the past few days. If Smooth hadn't been tending to my sister and nephew at the hospital, I would've been sneaking over to Tierra's job or her house instead of being at the club doing my job and covering his as well.

Although it was difficult to hold back, I wasn't going to entertain life with Tierra just yet because I wasn't about to be no side nigga. Running into her at the hospital was planned, but I wasn't expecting to see my sister and Smooth when I arrived though. I thought I'd spend a little time with Tierra before I went looking for them, but that wasn't how shit worked out.

As I stood near my truck waiting for her to join me, I realized how excited I was to see her. When I saw her heading my way, my leg started twitching... not the left or right one either, but the third one. Don't get me wrong, sex wasn't the only thing I wanted from Tierra. If she decided to leave that nigga and try to make it work with me, I'd be down for that. But I wasn't going to push her about it. That had to be her decision because the last thing I wanted was for her to have any regrets; especially after all that she had been through.

As she walked over to me and I immediately took her in my arms and kissed her. "Mmmm," she moaned as I released her.

"I thought about doing that all day," I admitted.

"Is that right?"

"That is right."

Holding her close to me, I leaned against my truck and stared as she looked back at me nervously. Twisting to the side a bit, Tierra glanced around the parking lot then turned her attention back to me.

"Do you mind if we sit in your truck?" she asked.

"Not at all."

I popped the locks to my ride and opened the passenger's side for her. After she hopped in and I shut the door, I walked around and got in as well.

"So, how's Sammy?" I asked.

"He was testing, so when they brought him back, Tangi said she'd call me tomorrow."

"Well, Smooth said they may release him tomorrow."

"That would be great! I'm sure Tangi will be happy about that. I know that shit must be stressful for the two of them," Tierra said.

"I bet it is," I cosigned. "But enough about the two of them, what's up with you and I?"

She smiled shyly. "I don't know. What do you want to be up with us?"

I leaned over and kissed her. "That's what I want."

"I could see why you would want that," she smiled.

"Look Tierra, I don't want to push you to do anything you don't..."

"I need to have a conversation with Thaddeus."

"Don't discuss any of this with him if you aren't sure what you wanna do. I mean, once you open that door, it may be hard to close it," I warned.

"What I'm doing to him right now would hurt him if he found out. If I don't talk to him, I'm no better than Dallas when he was cheating on me!"

"I understand why you might feel that way. I just want you to be sure of what you want," I explained.

"Are you sure of what you want?"

"Very sure."

"Well, I need to have that talk with Thaddeus as soon as possible," she assured.

"What are you going to tell him?"

"I don't know. What I do know is that I can't and won't string either of you along. That's not fair to you or him."

"Shit, you ain't finna string me along!" I enlightened with a chuckle. "But anyway, when are you going to have this 'talk' with him?"

"Probably in the morning. I mean, he shouldn't be too hurt about it considering everything that's been going on between us lately. Honestly, he can just go back to his baby mama!"

"See, now here you go." I laughed as we drove down the main street that led to my place.

"No, seriously. I swear he still has feelings for the chick and he's not gonna admit it, so I'm gonna confront him about it and see where it goes."

"So that's your game plan huh?" I clowned.

"Well, truthfully, I'm gonna ask for space because that's what I need. I'm not ready to marry him right now and he needs to know that."

"So, what are you ready for?" I teased trying to get a reaction out of her.

"Whatever it is you're dishing out this evening."

"Oh, you hungry?" I laughed glancing back and forth between her and the road ahead of me.

"Not for food," she flirted as she placed her hand on my upper thigh and began rubbing it.

"See, now yo ass is really starting something!" I warned as I adjusted my semi hard dick. It was quickly rising again thanks to the softness of her hand.

"Don't worry, I can surely finish it," she giggled as we pulled up to my house.

Being the gentleman that I was, I parked, let her out and escorted her inside. She slid off her shoes at the front door and followed me to my bedroom where we got comfortable.

"You want something to drink?" I offered, even though I knew I shouldn't have. The first time she and I got nasty, she was drunker than Ned the Wino from the show *Good Times*. Tonight, I wanted her to be sober for everything that was about to go down.

"Sure," she smiled as she laid across the top of my bed and propped her head up on my king-sized pillow.

After hooking us up with some Washington Red Apple Martini's using Crown Royal, Apple Puckers and cranberry juice, we drank and began fooling around. I had never been so comfortable around a female like I was around Tierra. That shit was crazy to me.

"Damn!" I sighed with a smile.

"What's wrong?"

"Shit, ain't nothing wrong. Quite the contrary, everything is so fuckin' right," I told her while leaning over to kiss her.

Taking the empty glass out of her hand, I set it on the nightstand then began to show Tierra my foreplay skills. Had her ass reaching for shit that wasn't even there!

"What the hell?!" she screamed out as I swirled my tongue around her clit as I gently finger fucked her into her first climax.

Switching it up, Tierra surprised me by reversing our position into a 69! I couldn't believe how that girl could suck the hell out of a dick! She almost made me cum in her mouth and had a nigga yelling out her damn name!

Coming up for air, Tierra smiled and climbed on top of my stiff erection. "Damn baby, you hard as a rock!"

"You got me like this baby!" I panted as I gripped her hips and matched her every thrust.

As our bodies connected, we stared into each other's eyes. This shit right here was so different for me because I had never done no shit like that. I barely wanted to see a bitch when I was fucking her. At least not her face...

"Oh, shit!" she screamed not taking her gaze off me. "I'm about to cum baby!"

"Me too!" I confessed as I bit down on my bottom lip and gave her all I had.

As our eyes continued to lock, we both released together. Then came the joyous smiles across our faces.

"You make me feel so fuckin' good Jay!" Tierra admitted as she rolled off me and into my arms. "I feel like I can truly be myself with you... no frontin', no playing games. Just be natural, ya know?"

"Shit, I know exactly whatchu talkin' bout. You got me over here stuck on stupid over you too," I blurted out without thinking first. The last thing I wanted was Tierra to know how hard I was falling for her. It was just like when we were younger, and I was too shy to push up on her like I wanted to. Now, it was definitely something different...

CHAPTER ELEVEN

Thaddeus

See that was that bullshit I was talking about! Tierra had the nerve to try me again and stay out all night. I didn't know what the fuck she was up to, but when she came waltzing her ass back home at five in the morning that was it! I was already dressed and ready to get up out of there. No way was I going to sit up there and be made a fool of the way that Dallas did her!

"I'm done playing this game with you Tierra!" I snapped as she walked in the door, went straight to the bedroom and changed into some pajamas. I was right on the back of her damn heels sniffing her ass out.

This time she didn't smell like liquor and cologne. This time she smelled like she had just taken a shower. I swear I was ready to choke her ass out.

"Oh, I'm not the one playing games!" she said calmly as she left the room and headed for the nursery to check on Miracle. Once again, I was right behind her.

"Yes, you are Tierra!" I said in a loud whisper.

"How long has she been asleep?"

"I just fed her, changed her and she's been knocked out about 20 minutes, but that's beside the point! While you're tryna sidestep all my fuckin' questions, tell me where the hell you been, Tierra!"

"I told you I went to the hospital..."

"Until five in the fuckin' morning?!"

"Look, you ain't gonna keep standing here cussing me out like that! I ain't cussed at you once but keep it up. You about to open up a whole can of shit I know you ain't ready for." She spoke calmly before going back into the bedroom. She must've noticed my bag packed on the floor by the door because when I walked in the room behind her she stared down at the duffle then up at me.

"You wanna tell me something?" she sighed as she folded her arms and rested them on her chest.

"Yeah, I'm leaving until you wanna tell me what's going on with you..."

"Nah, you ain't gonna flip this shit on me Thaddeus! You're the one that started this shit by texting that bitch nonstop the past couple of days!"

Now I was the one standing there looking real stupid. That shit right there caught me totally off guard and I wasn't prepared, so I didn't have a quick comeback! That showed the guilt that was written all over my face. I couldn't even deny that shit.

"What? I can't hear you Thaddeus!" she said as she cupped her hand over her right ear. "Don't you have something to say about that shit?!" she huffed boldly as she got in my personal space.

Staring down at her, I shook my head. "That wasn't shit. We were just kicking it about old times..."

"And she made it clear that she hadn't gotten over you Thaddeus and yet you still kept texting her back!"

Tierra was right, but I wasn't about to admit that shit and have her flip the argument back on me after the stunts she had been pulling! She had me fucked up. I may have been wrong for texting my ex like that, but it wasn't shit compared to Tierra staying out all night two nights in a row.

"Just as I thought Thaddeus!" she yelled, bent down, grabbed my bag then handed it to me. "Go ahead on and run to that bitch and YOUR son. Me and MY daughter will be just fine!"

Tierra was really hitting below the belt now! She knew that I loved Miracle with all my heart, just like she was my own flesh and blood. I don't even know why she was trying me right now.

"I don't give a fuck what you and I go through, Miracle will always be my baby girl. I've been here for both you and her since the day she was born, so don't even try it!" I told her before turning toward the door.

Without chasing behind me or trying to stop me from leaving, Tierra stood in the hallway with her cell in her hand. She didn't even wait for me to shut the front door before she started giggling and talking on the phone. I guess that was what she wanted all along.

To be honest, I'm very surprised by how she treated me. You would think after the way her ex had treated her she wouldn't do someone else that way. I swear right now she had me feeling like a disposable drinking cup. That shit hurt.

I had done everything I could to be there for her when that nigga was shitting on her... and with her best friend at that. When she and Tangi fell out, I was the one holding her hand and comforting her while she cried on my shoulder. Even while she had been sleeping out those two nights, I had been the responsible parent taking care of Miracle. What had even happened to us? Just two weeks ago, we were happy and making plans to get married. Now, I was on my way out with a bag in hand.

"Damn! Is she just throwing away this past year like it wasn't shit?" I wondered out loud as I got in my truck and backed out of the driveway, heading to my house.

Not getting two blocks down the road, my cell began to ring. I hoped it was Tierra with an apology, so without even bothering to check the screen, I answered it.

"Hey Thaddeus. I didn't mean to call you this early, but after talking to you last night I was worried about you."

"Nah, it's cool. I'm cool," I lied. Shit, my heart was fucked up behind Tierra. She and Miracle were my world. I couldn't even imagine life without them. I knew I should've just married her when we had planned it months ago. Now I may have waited too long...

"Thaddeus?!" Sheena yelled out. "Did you hear me?"

"Nah, my bad. What'd you say?"

"I said that I was dropping our son off at my cousin's house. They're going camping for the weekend."

"Oh, that's cool," I ignored that she said 'our son' because thoughts of Tierra were still invading my head.

"Well, I wanted to see you today so that we could sit down and talk, but I see you're preoccupied with something else..."

"No, no, I'm cool..."

"See, everything you say is cool. It's obvious that something has you distracted."

"Sheena, just come by in about an hour. We need to chop it up about the paternity test anyway."

"Okay, I'll see you then."

When I hung up, I was already pulling up to my place. I went in and poured myself a drink. I usually didn't consume alcohol that early in the morning, but on this day, I needed that shit.

One shot turned into two and two into three. By the fourth one, my ass was lit, and my doorbell was ringing.

Assuming it was Sheena, I swung the door open smiling. She just shook her head and brushed by me.

"Yo ass is in here fucked up at this time of morning Thaddeus?" she laughed and picked up the half empty fifth of Hennessey. "No glass or nothing huh?"

"Nah, I'm cool."

"Here you go again with that cool shit," she smirked and came over to me. Lifting her hand up to my face, Sheena swiped her palm against my neatly trimmed facial hair. "Damn, yo' ass is still fine."

"And so are you," I admitted without holding back.

It wasn't that I was interested in being in a relationship with Sheena, but she was beautiful and thick in all the right places. She stood right in front of me and her perfume mixed with the alcohol I consumed was turning me on.

"Since you don't wanna talk about what you're going through, let me help take your mind off it for a little while?" she offered while flirtatiously stroking my chest.

Boldly dropping my gym shorts to the floor, I slowly extended my hand out to palm the back of Sheena's head. "You sure can."

Taking the lead, she dropped to her knees and sucked my dick so good that I almost shot my kids down her throat. After continuing to pleasure me for the next few minutes, Sheena cut it short as she stood up and smiled. Coming out all her clothes and all that. She even began whispering about how she wanted me to make love to her. Oh, hell nah! That's not what I had in mind. Making love wasn't on the menu, but fucking the shit out of her from behind was. That way I didn't have to see her face to remind me of who I was banging. I wasn't searching for a love connection. I just needed to nut out some frustration and that's just what I did and was absolutely emotionless about the whole thing.

"Damn, that's not how I pictured it going down Thaddeus. I didn't even get to..."

"Yeah, it was a quick stress reliever and I appreciate it, but what we really need to do is call and make that appointment." I reminded as I checked the time while I washed my dick off and threw her the wet soapy rag. She was pissed.

"What the fuck Thaddeus?!" she screamed. "We hook up for the first time in five years and this is how you make love to me?"

"Make love?" I laughed. "No disrespect baby, but that was a straight fuck. No feelings attached."

"Wow!" she said rushing to throw her clothes on. "Fuck this shit and fuck you too Thaddeus!"

"Nah, already did that shit and it was way wilder than I remember, if that makes you feel any better..."

"What the hell?!" she yelled as she started tugging, scratching and swinging on me. I tried to block her blows, but I was still a little fucked up off the Hennessey.

"Stop! Yo ass is trippin'!" I huffed while getting her up off me and backing her ass up with a shove. "I dicked you down real good and you go to the left?! Shit, you should be thanking me because I know that shit was good. Had yo ass hollering out and shit. Truthfully, I pleasured you with this dick when I didn't have to give yo ass none."

"You're an asshole!" Sheena hollered as she straightened up her clothes and went for the door.

"Wait, wait! Come back here! We need to make this appointment!" I snapped loudly as I chased behind her in my boxer briefs all the way outside. My dick was still semi-hard, and it was bulging through enough to get the chick's attention that was walking her dog down the street. The way she glanced from my dick to my face with her mouth hanging open told it all. I just laughed and took my ass back in the house.

"That bitch is crazy!" I sighed as I sobered up enough to realize that I didn't use a condom when I fucked Sheena.

Now, I was the crazy one!

CHAPTER TWELVE

Tangi

Two days later...

Finally getting Sammy home and settling him in the crib with his breathing machine, I sighed in relief. It felt so good to be home.

"You get some sleep baby. I have some work to do on the computer so I'm gonna bring my laptop in here so I can keep an eye on Sammy."

"He's fine Smooth. We have the monitors set up and if his breathing becomes irregular the alarm will go off," I explained, but he wasn't going for it. He wanted to stay in the nursery and that's just where I left him.

Going to the bedroom, I got my cell and checked my messages. I only had one and it was from Tierra. After reading it, I dialed her up right away.

"Girl, what's up? Did he really pack a bag and leave?" I gasped not believing that she and Thaddeus had split up. "You told him?"

"I didn't have to tell him shit because when I walked in after staying out all night again, he was done. His bag was already packed, so why tell him shit?" Tierra explained.

"Wait, wait, wait! You stayed out again?!" I shouted.

"Hush, I'm grown damnit!" She laughed like she had done no wrong.

"So, you're really done with Thaddeus?"

"Shit, seems like we're done with each other."

"Wow! So, you're really digging my brother like that?" I pressed trying to figure out how they ended up fucking around in the first place.

"Yeah, I'm really feeling him."

"Tell the truth now Tierra... is this the first time y'all hooked up?"

"Yes!" she screamed. "I mean, he used to always flirt with me, but it just never was the right time..."

"So, how is now the right time?" I snapped playfully. "You were in a whole relationship with Thaddeus when you went and jumped on my brother's dick!"

"Hush heffa!" she laughed. "I did not confirm that we fucked lil' girl!"

"Deny it if you want to, but I know both of you and y'all fuckin'!" I pressed trying to get Tierra to admit to it.

"Now what the hell is that supposed to mean?"

"Nothing, just be honest and tell me the truth. Are you and Jay fooling around?"

"Yes, okay, yes!" she giggled loudly.

I guess I was being way too loud because before I knew it, Smooth came in the room and gave me a funny look. I wasn't sure how much he heard, but I was sure he heard part of it.

"What?" I asked him while I pushed the mute button. Tierra was talking so much that she didn't realize that I wasn't even listening.

"I know I didn't hear what I think I heard?"

"What do you think you heard?" I questioned playing his game.

"Did you say Tierra and Jay are fuckin' around?" Smooth asked with a raised brow.

"No, now mind ya business!" I clowned making him laugh.

Smooth shook his head. "I know what I heard and y'all are wilding the hell out. I guess ain't nobody learned from the shit that happened with you and Dallas."

Now that nigga had touched a nerve. I had to hang up on Tierra and cuss his ass out real quick.

"I know what I did was fucked up, but that gives you no right to keep throwing that shit up in my face! See, that's why we can't get along for five damn minutes..."

"I'm sorry. I didn't mean it like that," Smooth interrupted and came over to hug me. I really needed it and it helped calm me and the situation down. Just his touch was enough. It was his mouth that I couldn't deal with.

"I'm sorry too, but you know that's a touchy subject that will never sit well with me baby." I told him as I squeezed him back.

My mood was all over the place and the doctor was blaming it on some shit called postpartum depression. Hell, it didn't feel like I was depressed. It was more like mad, sad, happy and crazy. It was some shit I had no control over.

"Baby, try to take the meds that the doctor prescribed you. They may help you relax and not get so uptight," Smooth suggested.

Taking his advice, I got up and went to get my pills while he got me some juice to take it with. After gulping them down, I got in the bed and closed my eyes. Smooth climbed in with me.

At first, I was feeling irritated by his touch. It was even hard for me to just lay there and let him hold me, but I forced myself to. But, after the meds kicked in about twenty minutes later, I began feeling like I had smoked a blunt to the face. I was so high that I couldn't stop laughing. I was even getting frisky. That was right up Smooth's alley!

He was lucky that morning and he had the medicine to thank for that because I put it on him and put his ass to sleep. I would've gone with him, but by the time I took a quick shower, Sammy was fussing.

Letting Smooth sleep, I went in and fed my son and checked all the connections on his breathing machine. Sammy was just up smiling, even with all that crap hooked up to him, he was still a happy baby.

After he burped a good three times and I changed him, he went right back to sleep. I laid him in his crib and went to my room to cuddle under Smooth. That was where we stayed until just before noon.

Ring, ring, ring!!

"Baby, it's your phone! It's been ringing for a minute now. Can you please get it?" I moaned rolling over to put the pillow over my face. I was so tired I could barely move.

I hadn't realized how tired I was from taking care of a sick baby for the last week. I kept thinking that this was all my fault. I had done so much shit in my past including fucking Dallas behind my best friend's back, that I knew this was my karma. Not to mention getting rid of my first baby. That shit always sat in the back of my mind that this was my punishment for doing that. There were so many things I wished I could take back and do over. I'm not sure if I would've gone through with the pregnancy, but I definitely wouldn't have taken that shit to terminate it myself.

At the time, I wasn't in my right frame of mind. All I wanted was to erase Dallas from my thoughts and life. I didn't want to carry his child and he had already followed me to the women's clinic where I was getting the pregnancy terminated and stopped me. What was I supposed to do? I had to do it myself!

As much as I tried to put that out of my head, it constantly replayed itself over and over again. "I'm sorry," I cried to the blurred vision of the lost baby in my dreams as I tossed and turned in my bed. "I didn't want to get rid of you that way, but I had no choice after your stupid daddy had dragged me out of the clinic. Ugh! I really hated Dallas." The dream seemed so real.

As the blurry image floated away, I saw myself crying for that baby. I began reaching out, but nothing was there. I couldn't feel anything except for my body lightly shuddering from side to side.

"Tangi! Tangi!" I heard someone calling my name as my body continued shaking.

As the nudges became harder, I was finally able to force my eyes to open. Squinting from the bright light from the sun, I struggled to focus on the person standing over me. It took several moments for my head to stop spinning and I was able to see Smooth's face.

Oh, shit, he don't look happy!

"What?" I whispered in a total state of confusion.

"You were talking in your sleep!"

"So?" I huffed as I hugged my pillow and closed my eyes to go back to sleep.

"Nah man! You gotta get the hell up! We need to talk about this shit!" Smooth demanded angrily.

"Talk about what Samuel? I'm exhausted!"

Yes, I called him by his government name because all I wanted was for him to go away and let me sleep. Why the hell was he pestering me anyway? We could talk about whatever he wanted to talk about when I woke up later.

"Why don't you go check on Sammy?" I whined. "I need just a couple more..."

"Aw, hell naw! Get up Tangi!" he fumed.

Damn! What the hell could be so important about me talking in my fucking sleep?

Opening my eyes once again, I sat up in bed trying to focus on Smooth and feel him out. He seemed really upset, but I didn't know about what.

As I continually stared at him, I could swear there was smoke coming out of his ears. "What's your problem Samuel? You said that I could get some rest, so I don't understand why the hell you're standing over me like you have a fucking issue with me that can't wait?!"

"I do have a fucking issue, a problem or whatever you wanna call it!" he spat through tightly clinched teeth. "We need to talk to about when you had the miscarriage right now Tangi!"

"What?! Aw hell naw!" I laid back down in the bed and buried myself in the covers again. "I'm tired as fuck and here you go trying to talk about some shit from the past!"

"Tangi I'm not playing with you! You need to get up so we can talk about this shit right the hell now!"

Smooth had me fucked up if he thought I was going to wake up and talk about that shit! I kept trying to forget about that whole episode. Why the hell was he bringing it up now?

"We can talk about this when I wake up!"

"Hell naw! We gon' talk about that shit right now or I won't be here when you wake up!" he threatened.

What the hell was this boy talking about? He won't be here when I wake up? Well, where the fuck was he gonna be then? As much as I didn't want to get up now, I had no choice. Once again, I sat up in bed and glared at Smooth.

"Okay fuck it! Since you won't leave me alone, go ahead say it! Tell me what's so damn important that you have to talk to me about it right this damn minute!"

"I wanna talk about when you lost the baby... you said that it was my child." He paused.

"And? What about it?" I pressed wanting him to get to the damn point so I could get some sleep. I was delirious!

"Well, when you were talking in your sleep you said something about '*I'm sorry, I didn't mean to get rid of you that way, but I had no choice'*..." Smooth poorly imitated my voice then smirked.

"What? That's crazy! I never said that!" I said as I tried to laugh it off as everything slowly began to come back to me.

All that shit I was saying in my dream, Smooth was now confronting me with. Sure, I knew I had said it, but I thought I was saying it in my dream to the blurred baby image.

Did I really say that shit out loud?!

The implications of what Smooth may have heard had my heart pounding so hard, I could hear the thumps.

No, I couldn't have said that shit out loud!

"That's not all you said. You said that the crazy daddy Dallas had dragged you out of the clinic before you could abort the baby and that you hated him for it! So, you wanna tell me what that was about?" he growled coming up on me like he wanted to put paws on me.

"I-I-I-I don't know. I must have been having some kind of nightmare…"

"About Dallas? About a baby you were carrying for him? Why would you have any kind of dream about *his baby* if the baby was mine?" he asked.

"I'm not sure, but…"

"Tangi, I need you to tell me the truth. I need you to look me in my fuckin' eye and keep it real with me. Do you even know what the truth is anymore, or have you been lying for so long that you forgot how to tell the truth?"

"Okay, now listen here. I may have been sleeping and shit when I said what I said, but I'm not gonna let you stand here and insult my character this way…"

"Your character? Insult your character? What kind of character would that be exactly? Is that the same character that smiled in her best friend's face while she was banging her husband behind her back? Is that the same character that caused you to look me in the eye and lie about going to some clinic to try to abort the baby? What character are we talking about Tangi? Because it seems to me that you've been lying ever since the first day that I met your ass!" he yelled out at me in an angered tone that had me a little scared.

Not only did that nigga have me nervous, the shit he was saying to me hurt like hell. He was telling the truth though. I had lied to him for a long time. I didn't mean to, but I couldn't help it. Now he was standing there glaring at me because I spoke some truth while I was asleep.

Oh my God! I'm gonna sue that fucking doctor for prescribing me those bullshit meds. None of this would've ever happened if I wasn't on that shit!

Now I was sitting there looking dumb. I didn't even know what to say because he would know that I was lying.

As the tears began streaming from my eyes, I contemplated telling him that it was just a bad dream that I was fighting. But at the end of the day, I couldn't keep lying about this. God was obviously trying to make me tell the truth, so I had to follow his lead.

Whatever happens after this... must be God's will.

"Fine Smooth! I wasn't honest about the baby being yours, or the miscarriage," I confessed as I watched his facial expression just collapse into sadness. I jumped out of bed and rushed over to him because I needed him to understand why I did what I did. "Please listen to me..." I reached for his hand, but he jerked it from me.

"Listen to you? All this time, you had me taking care of you and loving you and the whole time you were lying to my face! Why would you do that Tangi?" The tone in his voice sounded so hurt as tears sprung to his eyes.

"I didn't mean to lie to you. I really thought the baby was yours, but then I found out that I was further along and knew that it was Dallas' baby! I couldn't have his baby. It would've ruined everything... my relationship with you, my friendship with Tierra..."

"So, what did you do? Did you terminate the pregnancy at the clinic or did Dallas drag you out before that could happen?"

"I went to the clinic to terminate the pregnancy, but somehow, he found out that I was there, so yes. He came in and dragged me outside. We had a whole fight in the parking lot. After he shoved me to the ground I started screaming for someone to call the police and he took off."

"So, the day you had the miscarriage, what happened? Did you lose the baby from that fall? When Dallas pushed you?" he asked.

"No, and that's why I took some stuff to make the baby pass..."

"*What do you mean pass?!*"

"To kill it!"

"So, you purposely miscarried?! You purposely killed the baby you were carrying?!"

"Yes."

The disgusted look on his face as he glared at me had me worried. I wondered if he'd be able to forgive me for that betrayal. I wondered if we'd ever be able to get past this.

"Why didn't you just tell me the truth?"

"I didn't want you to look at me the way you are right now," I said with tears flowing from my eyes. "I'm so sorry..."

Reaching out helplessly towards him, he pulled back once again. I watched as he walked to the closet and grabbed a duffle bag. Then I saw him begin to put socks and underwear in it. He walked in the bathroom and grabbed his toothbrush and toiletries.

"What are you doing?" I asked nervously.

"I'm leaving..."

"No, you can't leave me! I'm sorry I didn't tell you the truth, but I was afraid of losing you!" I cried as I tried to get him to stop packing and listen to me.

"We could've had it all Tangi. A wonderful life. A perfect family. I love you so much, but I won't be with a woman who can't be honest with me. As much as I love you baby, I can't be with you," he said with tears flowing down his cheeks.

"Please don't leave me! I need you! We can work through it and get past this!" I begged.

"We can't work through shit because I'm never gonna be able to trust you! You lied to me from the first day I introduced myself. I can't be with a woman like that. I'll take care of my son, but you and I are done!"

"Noooooo!" I cried as I held on to him for dear life. "It can't just be over like that! You have to give me another chance!"

"I've given you chance after chance. I'm fresh out of those..."

"We have to try for Sammy..."

"Don't you ever pull our son into our shit like some pawn! You should've been honest," he said as he grabbed his shit and headed out the bedroom door.

I ran after him, crying and sniffling while snot and tears mixed together. I was trying not to wake the baby, but I needed Smooth to listen to me. I needed him to stay with me. I couldn't take care of our sick baby by myself.

"PLEASE DON'T LEAVE ME!!" I begged as I tried to keep him from walking out of the house.

"Tangi let me go! No matter how much you beg, it's not happening."

"Then you never loved me!"

"Shit, you probably never loved me! Look, I gotta go!" I shrugged her off me and pushed open the door that led to outside.

I can't believe this shit even happened. How the hell did I get so loose in the lips?

CHAPTER THIRTEEN

Smooth

Nah, fuck all that shit! I loved Tangi with all my heart, but I'd be damn if I allowed that woman to play me like that. I couldn't believe the words that were coming out of her mouth while she was sleeping. I thought for sure that I had misunderstood, especially when she said that the baby's daddy had dragged her outside the clinic. I knew I hadn't been to no clinic, so I thought she was having some kind of nightmare, but that was it... until she mumbled Dallas' name. That's when I knew that she was telling the truth.

I would've liked to just forget about what I heard, but I couldn't. Tangi had been consistently lying to me ever since we met. I couldn't be with a woman like her. I had never gone through so much trouble just to love a woman. All I wanted was to be with her and my son, but she had fucked all that up and there was no coming back for what I thought we had.

Tangi truly brought this shit on herself!

As I placed my bags in the truck, I watched her standing in the doorway crying. At this point, those tears didn't mean shit to me. That's how she always got me… with the puppy dog eyes and crocodile tears. I watched as she crumbled to the floor bawling, but I couldn't let her con me again.

Hopping in the driver's seat, I started the truck and backed out the driveway headed back to my own crib until I remembered that I had put in on the market and moved all my belongings to storage. From Tangi's past actions, I should've known that I'd end up needing my own spot again.

Damn! I really thought I was gonna marry that girl. I thought we'd have a couple of more kids. I thought we'd have the life I always dreamed about.

Now I know better.

As I wiped my tears with the back of my hand, I headed on over to the Hilton that was right down the street from the club. Sure, I had the money to stay in a hotel for a year, but that's not where I wanted to be. I had to find another house and fast.

Dammit! I did not see this shit coming, especially not on the first day that we brought our son home!

Temporarily dismissing all the ill feelings, I went and checked into the hotel then went right to sleep. After all that shit, I was mentally exhausted.

"Ugh!" I grunted as I stretched and checked my cell for the time. It was well after ten at night and I had twelve new text messages from Tangi... all of which I ignored. Instead of responding to her, I took my ass to the bathroom and hopped in the shower, changed my clothes and went down to the club. It wasn't my night to work, but I needed a drink and wanted to talk to Jay about his sister before she called him and told him her version.

Shit, I already knew how protective he was of her, so I knew if she told her version first, he'd be salty with me before hearing my side.

Making it down there an hour later, I found Tierra's dude sitting at a table near the bar getting fucked up. I guess I wasn't the only one having trouble at home. After ordering a double shot from the bartender, I went over and began chopping it up with ol' boy.

"Aye! Thaddeus, right?" I asked when he looked up at me through glazed eyes. "Mind if I join you?"

"No, not at all. What's up Smooth?" he sneered and downed his drink before setting his empty glass beside the three other ones. "I guess Tierra told ya girl what happened huh?"

"Happened with what?"

"I had to walk out on Tierra and lucky I still had my old place!"

"What? What happened?"

"Yeah, I didn't have a choice. Shit I wasn't about to stay there and let her keep stepping out on me like I wasn't shit. You know she stayed out all night two times?! Came home smelling like some other nigga, booze and sex." He sighed like he was really in his feelings.

Damn! Every time somebody thought they had it bad, there was always somebody who had it worse. I never thought Tierra was capable of doing some shit like that to this nigga. I thought she was in love with him.

"Nah man. I'm sorry to hear that. Tangi hadn't told me shit because I just walked out on her ass too and you're the lucky one alright. My ass put my house on the market when I moved in with her. I had to get a damn suite at the Hilton down the road," I confessed as I finished my drink and waved over at the waitress, Beatrice.

"Now that's fucked up man. What happened between y'all?" he asked then assumed we were both having the same problems. "Don't tell me her ass is cheating too?"

"Nah, her ass just doing the same shit as always... lying her ass off when she didn't have to."

"Yeah, Tierra lied too. Lied about fuckin' with another nigga."

Suddenly it came to me soon as Jay approached the table. I remembered what I overheard Tangi saying to Tierra over the phone.

"What's up Jay?" I said dapping him up.

Jay then reached over to pound fists with Thaddeus. I watched closely as Thaddeus' nostrils widened as Jay drew back. He immediately turned his face up and ordered another drink from Beatrice who was now standing there waiting.

"All this shit is on me..."

"Nah, I got this," Thaddeus insisted pulling out his platinum card.

Standing down, Jay laughed and boldly took a seat with us. I mean, what the fuck could Thaddeus do? We were inside Jay's club. He owned that shit and controlled everything that was going on inside. I just prayed that Thaddeus was smart and sober enough to realize that shit.

"So, why you both over here lookin' like y'all niggas havin' a fuckin' pity party?" Jay clowned as he sipped slowly on his drink. I knew that fool all too well. He was on point.

"My bitch cheating and his bitch lyin'..."

"Whoa nigga! That woman you callin' a bitch is my sister," Jay warned in a low tone.

Scooting my chair back and planting my feet firmly on the floor, I got ready for whatever. These two were some big niggas. Not fat at all, but both were tall and muscular.

"I know exactly who she is. How the fuck you think I got shot? All behind that bullshit affair your sister had with Tierra's husband."

Now Thaddeus was pushing it. I could tell from the throbbing temples that Jay was getting mad. He was trying to remain calm, but I could see the rage was building. I wanted to warn Thaddeus about playing it safe, but he had already been drinking so... I just prepared myself for the fall out.

"You harpin' on some old shit dude. Don't blame your problems at home on what happened in the past. That shit happened before you even came in the fuckin' picture!" Jay shot nastily and stood up.

Thaddeus stood, then I did. I wasn't about to let this fight go down up in the club. After all, this was a place of business and there were people up in here.

"Nigga you right, but I'm here now." Thaddeus wasn't backing down.

"I'm gonna give yo ass a pass because I know yo ass is drunk right now. Plus, I see somebody else already done put it on you by all those scratches and bruises on yo face and neck. Why don't you try healing from yo last ass whoopin' before askin' for another?"

Thaddeus lunged toward Jay before I could get between them and those niggas started scrapping. I didn't even have to intervene because Jay had beat his ass and security was tossing Thaddeus out within minutes.

"Damn! What the fuck was that all about?" I asked Jay as he swiped his hands down his black slacks and straightened out his collar on his blue button-down shirt.

"You saw that nigga lunge at me, right? I wasn't about to let that fool steal on me! Especially up in my own shit!" Jay huffed as smoke spewed from his ears.

"Yeah, I seen that shit, but why was ol' boy comin' for you like that?" I pressed trying to get that nigga to admit that he was fucking with Tierra. Even if he didn't admit it though, from what I saw and heard the other night, I already knew what was up between the two of them.

"He's obviously mad about something. Shit, instead of trying to swing on me, the nigga should've just come off the chest and said the shit..."

"What shit?" I laughed looking him straight in the face.

"I should've known, my sister got a big ass mouth!" Jay shook his head and got us some fresh drinks since the other ones got knocked off the table during the scuffle he had with Thaddeus.

As we sat there for the next hour, we talked about his newfound relationship with Tierra. I was finally able to get in a damn word about Tangi. "You know me and your sister got into it today."

"About what now nigga?" Jay sighed deeply like he wasn't surprised.

After explaining everything that had happened, he was just as appalled as I was. He even apologized for his sister.

"I can't believe that girl. She ain't been the same since all that shit came out about her and Dallas. She's been acting reckless and she has to be held accountable for that shit."

Thinking about what the nurse said at the hospital, I shared it with Jay. Now he was really tripping.

"They got her ass on meds for that shit?!"

"Yeah, you just ain't seen her man. She's happy one minute and ready to fight a nigga the next. One minute she's giggling and the next she's crying. But the fucked up thing about it is, she's been lying since day one and that's what got me. I can't be with somebody I can't trust."

"I feel you man, but the baby. Y'all got lil' Sammy and right now he's going through all these medical issues and shit..."

"Oh, I got that. I'm gonna be right there to help her. We just gotta figure out some type of schedule because I'm not moving back over there."

"Well, I just hope everything works out," Jay said while checking his phone as he stood up from the table. "I'm about to go in the office and take this shit. I know this girl might be trippin' off me dusting her dude off."

"That must be Tierra."

Without answering me verbally, Jay just smiled and disappeared in the back. All I could do is shake my head at the whole situation. Right now, it seemed like everyone was running to somebody else when they had problems at home. That was something that I wasn't about to do.

Sure, sex was good. One of the best feelings in the world was to climax with someone you loved. That wasn't important to me right then though. What mattered to me was my son and my fucking sanity while dealing with Tangi, I had to be smart and think with my upper head.

Unlike them other niggas, I know that fucking the next bitch won't eliminate my problems. That shit right there will only create more...

CHAPTER FOURTEEN

Tierra

When I got that call from Thaddeus, he was slurring his words. I could barely understand him telling me that he and Jay had just gotten into a fight. That shit had me riled up, but what piped me right back down was when he told me that he knew it was Jay that I was messing around with.

Hell yeah, I denied that shit as best as I could, but when he said that Jay was wearing the same cologne that he smelled on me that morning I stayed out all night, my ass got to stuttering.

"Huh? What? Ah, ah, a million men probably wear that shit! You can't just pin that shit on me!" I yelled through the phone.

"Prove that shit! I'm right down the damn street. I want you to call that nigga in front of me and prove you ain't fuckin' with him!"

"I ain't doin' that high school bullshit! We ain't no fuckin' kids!" I shot at him for suggesting such nonsense. "You gotta be fucking drunk and you betta not come over here acting crazy. Maybe we should have this conversation tomorrow after you sleep that shit off!"

"I don't need to sleep shit off, now open the fuckin' door before I use my key!" he threatened. Now my ass was scared. This nigga was not only mad, but he was extremely intoxicated and that was a dangerous mix.

"I'm calling the police right now!" I threatened as I dialed Jay on my other line. I was so damn nervous that I wound up hanging up on everyone.

My cell rang right back, and it was Jay. Soon as I said hello, Thaddeus was calling on the other line and beating on the door.

"What the fuck is going on over there?" Jay yelled trying to get my attention.

"It's Thaddeus! He's drunk and he done brought his ass over here! Now, he's beating on my damn door!"

"I'm on my way, but call the police baby! I'm 30 minutes away! Fuck!" Jay hissed. "You ain't got a pistol or taser or something?"

"No!" I screamed as the front door flew off the hinges.

"Where's Miracle?!" Jay asked trying to keep me on the phone as I went to the kitchen to find a knife.

"She's with my mother," I whispered.

Suddenly, I was snatched by the back of my hair and the phone flew out of my hand. Now I was totally helpless as I stared into Thaddeus' angry bloodshot eyes. He had me hemmed up against the pantry door.

As I hung with my feet dangling in the air, I observed all the marks on him, both old and new. It wasn't just Jay he had been fighting with. That was just the ammunition I needed to turn shit on him.

"Put me down and get your fuckin' hands off me Thaddeus! You're mad at me about some shit you know nothing about when you've been over there fuckin' on Sheena! You think I'm dumb? You think I don't know?"

Releasing his hold with guilt written all over his face, he came even closer to me. "You disgust me you know that? I gave you my all just for you to go fuck another nigga..."

"Get out of my face with all..."

WHAP!

Thaddeus backhanded me so hard that my body spun in a full circle before it went crashing against the grey tiled kitchen flooring. I swear I was seeing stars before everything went black.

<hr>

"Did that nigga just knock me out?!" I groaned in pain a while later as I pried myself from the floor while clinching my left cheek. "Did he seriously put his fuckin' hands on me?!"

I cried as I stood there not believing what had happened. That nigga had seriously struck me with a mighty blow, and I was bleeding from my mouth! I knew that because I could taste the blood.

"Tierra?!!" Jay hollered out flying through the front door and into the kitchen. "What the fuck happened. Did that nigga do this to you?"

"Yes, he knows about us."

"So, that gave him the right to put his hands on you?" Jay hissed as he wet a piece of paper towel and wiped the blood dripping from my swollen bottom lip. "I see he didn't learn his lesson! I'm gonna have to..."

"No Jay! I'm gonna call the cops. He kicked my door in and assaulted me in my home! That's a charge!"

"And that nigga got mail coming here and some of his shit is still here..."

"What about him hitting me?" I cried.

"Will it make you feel better to get him locked up for a night then sent to take anger management classes or me shutting that nigga down for good, so he won't mess with you again?"

"I don't want you to kill him Jay!" I hollered in fear that he was going to do some gangsta shit and put Thaddeus to sleep for good. I definitely didn't want that. We had suffered enough death.

"I'm not gonna do no dumb shit like that baby," Jay assured as he hugged me and stroked my back. "I know how to silence a muthafucka without killing him baby. Don't worry."

I told Jay I wasn't worried, even though I was. I mean, of course I wanted Thaddeus to pay for what he did to me, but not to that extreme and I knew how Jay got down. Although he was a very successful businessman, he was raised in the streets. That I knew for a fact.

Feeling secure in his arms, I rested my head on his chest as he assured me that everything would be okay. "Just come home with me Tierra. Miracle is good with your mother the next couple of days. That will give us some time to figure out what to do from here."

"Okay, but I can't leave my door like that."

"Don't worry about it. I have a toolbox in my truck. It's just the bottom bracket. I can fix it for now and have someone come out and repair it properly tomorrow."

"Thank you so much Jay. I honestly don't know what I would do without you tonight." I sniffled as I gently pecked his lips. "Ouch!"

"Yeah, he really fucked yo lip up baby," Jay teased playfully.

"That's so not funny!" I pouted.

"No, it's really not, but that nigga is gonna have his day..."

"You already fucked him up Jay!" I reminded.

"Yeah, alright. We're not gonna talk about that right now Tierra. Go pack a bag while I fix this door right quick."

Running off to my bedroom, I just started slinging shit into my overnight bag. It was already equipped with all the travel size personals that I needed, so all I had to do was get underclothes, pajamas and a few casual outfits. If I needed anything else, I would buy it the following day.

"I'm ready!" I chanted as I went outside to find Jay smoking a blunt while eyeing the perimeter of my property. He was so focused that he didn't even look at me until he finished his visual scan.

"Okay, let's go."

After he stepped back from the damaged door, he locked it and went and let me in the passenger's side then hopped in himself. As Jay backed out the driveway, my nerves calmed down quite a bit. As he drove down the street, my cell started going off.

"Don't tell me that nigga is calling after the shit he just pulled!" Jay huffed. "Let me answer that shit."

"No, he's only gonna act out more! I don't wanna have to watch my back everywhere I go! You see what that crazy muthafucka did already! I see now that I didn't know him at all when I decided to get involved with him. I really didn't think in a million years that he would have ever hit me!"

"Yeah, I guess we all underestimated him, but it won't happen again though! I can promise you that!" Jay responded as he reached for my ringing cell.

Tired of arguing and fighting, I just handed the phone over and let him answer it. I mean, shit was already messed up. What more damage could it do?

"Yeah, I think we have a problem playa," Jay said after connecting the call. He didn't have the call on speaker so I couldn't hear shit Thaddeus was saying back to him.

"All that shit don't amount to shit in my book playa, but best believe I'm gonna deal with you for putting your hands on Tierra," Jay paused for a few seconds before speaking again. "Save a ho'? Nigga miss me with them nursery rhymes and games you playin'..."

Jay was getting more upset by the minute. I really didn't want it to escalate, so I slowly stuck my hand out and grabbed the phone before hitting the 'end' button.

"Why the hell you do that baby?" Jay asked with a confused look.

"I just want to go to your house, take a shower and cuddle. I don't wanna think about nothing or nobody else but you," I purred in an effort to butter him up and get his mind on other things.

With a smile, Jay told me that he would try to let it go for the rest of the night and deal with it the following day. Boy, I should've known that was a lie because as soon as we got to his house and I got in the shower his ass left.

When I came out of the bathroom to an empty bedroom and saw my cell laying on the bed displaying Thaddeus' contact information, I knew shit was all bad. I knew Jay had gone to meet with him.

Dialing him up immediately to stop him from making a huge mistake, I got no answer. Instead, Jay hit me with a text telling me that he would be home soon. Although it brought worry to my mind, it brought warmth to my heart knowing that I was protected no matter what.

My hero! Why didn't I hook up with him years ago? Wow! He was right here in my face this whole time...

CHAPTER FIFTEEN

Jay

Tierra was a damn fool if she thought I wasn't gonna go handle that nigga for putting his hands on her. Soon as she took her ass in the bathroom and I heard the shower running, I called Thaddeus and told him to meet me back at the club. That pussy ass nigga wasn't about to do that shit. His scary ass wanted me to meet him at his 24-hour gym. That was cool too, but I wasn't nobody's fool. I dialed Smooth up to see if he could have my back. I didn't need him to come in with me. I just needed him to be close by in case Thaddeus and his brother was on some dirty shit. Yeah, a nigga did some research on that fool on my way over there. I always had to be two steps ahead.

"Nigga are you serious?" Smooth yelled into the phone. "He kicked in the door and busted her in the mouth like that?!"

"Hell yeah, and now I'm about to meet up with him," I explained. "I swear that nigga reminding me of that other fool Tierra was married to. If that muthafucka don't chill, he gon' be sleeping with the fishes just like Dallas' dumb ass!"

"Aye bro, we got away with that shit the first time, so we gon' chill on doing that shit again. I ain't trying to go to jail behind that bullshit!" he explained.

"I feel that man, but sometimes..."

"Nah, this ain't one of those times! You and that nigga need to talk that shit out! I mean, it ain't like they married or have any kids together. If it's over, it should just be over and they should go their separate ways," Smooth said.

"Right. And that's what she wants. She just wants to be free to do what she wants to do with me. She doesn't wanna have to be looking over her shoulder every time she sets foot outside the house," I said.

"I feel you on that. Make that nigga understand that you mean business!"

"Oh, that's exactly what I'm gonna do. So, you coming up here?" I asked just to be sure.

"Yea, I'm already on my way. I should be pulling up at the same time as you," he said.

"Okay, cool. You don't have to get out of the car. Just park where you can keep an eye out in case those fools try to jump me."

"Yea, I gotchu!"

I continued to drive while avoiding Tierra's phone calls. I knew she was gonna try to stop me from confronting that nigga, but he didn't leave me with a choice. I was raised in a household where men didn't raise their hands toward women. I would fuck any nigga up for putting their hands on my sister or mother. So, now that Tierra and I were starting something, I was gonna protect her too. Honestly, I should've been there for Tierra a long time ago. I mean, I had been feeling her since way back. I don't know why I didn't make a move since then. Things between us would've still been going strong and I know that because I know us.

"This nigga beat me here?!"

As I pulled into the gym parking lot, I spotted Smooth's truck. I wondered how he got here before I did, but I didn't spend too much time worrying about it. I was just glad to see that he hadn't let me down. I turned off my truck and stepped out, making sure to nod my head in Smooth's direction. Then I headed inside.

Striding in as cool as a cucumber, I wasn't worried about a damn thing. I was a street nigga and had been in worse scuffles than the one me and ol' boy got it earlier. He should've known that shit was coming though. You don't put your hands on a woman like that and think shit ain't gon' happen to you. Tierra wasn't only a woman, but she was Miracle's mother. If that muthafucka cared anything about the baby the way he claimed, he would've never struck her mother. I mean, he hit her pretty hard because her lip was busted, and her left cheek was swollen.

"Wassup," Thaddeus greeted as he drew me from my thoughts.

"Look man, I didn't come here for all these pleasantries and shit. I came to talk to you about what you did to Tierra," I enlightened him sternly. He needed to know right then that this wasn't no damn friendly visit. I was pissed.

"Let's take this to my office. There's no need for my customers to know anything about this."

"Shit, lead the way!" I sneered as he turned, and I followed behind him.

As I watched that nigga walk, I wondered what the hell Tierra ever saw in him. I mean, I know that I'm a dude and I'm attracted to women, but if I was a chick, I wouldn't want this nigga. Yeah that fool had upper body muscles and shit, but he was round in the middle and had chicken legs. In my eyes, he was shaped like Patrick, ya know SpongeBob's bestie? He walked like he had two thumbs up his ass or like he was constipated. As he opened the door to his office, I followed him inside.

"You can have a seat..."

"Nah, I'll stand if it's all the same to you."

"Suit yourself. So, you really fuckin' my bitch, huh?" he asked disrespectfully.

"I'd watch how you speak about Tierra. I mean, weren't you just loving on her and shit? Now, all of a sudden, she's a bitch!"

"Hell yea! If she wasn't happy with me, she should've broken up with me instead of fuckin' yo ass!"

"Okay, I can admit that maybe we were wrong for starting this thing while the two of you were still involved..."

"Uh, ya think?" he shot sarcastically.

"Yea, I just said we could've handled it better! That doesn't give you the right to put your hands on her in that way!" I repeated. "You're a man... a big ass fuckin' man! I don't know how you were raised, but apparently, I was raised differently. My parents taught me to love and protect women... not beat up on them!" I hissed.

"Whatever! You don't know shit about me or my upbringing..."

"I know you knocked Tierra out with that punch! I know her cheek is swollen, and her lip is busted! I know that!" I said as anger began to grow inside me even more. "You said you loved Tierra, but that ain't love!"

"Nigga, you probably would've done the same thing if she had fucked over you that way!"

"Never! I would never punch a woman like that! Only a coward ass nigga would do some shit like that..."

"Watch what you say about me, ma nigga!"

"Why? You think you gon' poke yo chest out and do me like you did Tierra? I promise you that you won't get the same outcome. I didn't come here to square up with you but if you want it, shit I got it for you!" I smiled, letting him know he wasn't intimidating me. "Now, I'ma say this one time and one time only. Stay away from Tierra and Miracle! She doesn't wanna be with you anymore, especially after what happened between y'all earlier. Y'all are done!"

"That's for her to say!" he said as he poked his chest out.

"Nah, it's for me to say and I said it! I know you think you some big bad man and shit, but I promise you that you don't want this! Don't put yourself in the same position that Dallas found himself in..." I threatened.

His face went blank for a minute and then it was like a lightbulb went off.

"It was you? You killed Dallas?" he gasped thinking he knew shit, but I wasn't admitting a damn thing.

"I didn't say that shit! Did you hear me say that?"

"Yea, you just said..."

"I said don't put yourself in the same position as him, meaning don't end up at the bottom of the bayou by acting stupid! I didn't say I put him there, but I ain't shedding no tears about his dead ass either!" I scoffed and turned my nose up while reminding myself that I had to watch what the fuck I said pertaining to that nigga in the future. What happened to Dallas wasn't something that I wanna go around telling everybody. I'd be damn if I was gonna end up in jail behind some shit that nigga caused.

"As I said, stay away from Tierra and Miracle."

"Miracle is my daughter..."

"No, she's not!" I said through clenched teeth.

"She's just as much my daughter as she is Tierra's. Just because it ain't my blood running through her veins..."

"And there it is! Miracle ain't your daughter! She's Tierra's daughter... period! She doesn't need your help raising her daughter anymore, ya feel me?"

"I'm not something you can just dispose of. I've been there for that little girl since day one! She's gonna miss me if I just drop out of her life!"

"She'll be fine. Trust me, I'll make damn sure Miracle and Tierra are good without you." I turned and headed for the door, then as an afterthought, I turned around again. "Take care man! Just remember to keep your distance from MY WOMAN and her baby girl!"

I turned around once again and walked out. I knew that he was pissed, but I bet he wouldn't do shit. That nigga didn't want none of this shit.

He better get the fuck on with that shit!

Exiting out of the building, I gave Smooth a thumbs up. He started his truck as I got in mine and we both left the parking lot. He called me as we went in opposite directions.

"What happened?"

"Shit! I just told him to stay away from Tierra and Miracle or he was gon' end up like Dallas!" I said.

"What? You told him that you killed Dallas?"

"No, I just told him to stay away or he'd find himself at the bottom of the bayou like Dallas did for acting stupid! Look, the bottom line is I told him to leave Tierra alone. I think I got through to him!" I said.

"Let's hope you didn't get through to him in a way that's gon' get us locked the fuck up!" Smooth huffed heavily.

"Nigga chill! Ain't nobody getting locked up!"

At least I hoped not...

CHAPTER SIXTEEN

Tangi

Two weeks later...

Things between Smooth and I hadn't gotten any better over these past couple of weeks. I only got to see him when he came by to help me with Sammy during the day, but by sunset he was gone again. I apologized to him several times, but nothing was working. I just couldn't seem to get him to come back to me this time. Last week, the doctors had finally taken Sammy off of the breathing machine. He still had to take breathing treatments twice a day, but at least he wasn't connected to the machine 24/7 anymore.

Since he was removed from the machine, he seemed to be a much happier baby. I know I was happy that I no longer had to monitor him all day every day anymore. My baby was finally able to breathe on his own without any help from that bullshit machine.

Waking up this morning to the sun peeking in from the blinds, a smile slowly crept across my face. I usually woke up when it was still dark because Sammy wanted a bottle.

Leaning over to the right side, I reached for my phone to check the time. I was surprised that it was almost ten o'clock and my baby hadn't woken me up yet. Something definitely wasn't right.

Flying out of bed barefooted, I rushed to check on him. With every stride, the panic inside me became stronger causing me to pick up the pace. I was practically running by the time I made it to the nursery.

"Hey baby boy!" I huffed as I made it to the crib then looked down. "Ooooooo..."

My heart dropped to see that my baby wasn't moving. His little chest wasn't going up and down either.

"Sammy!" I called out as I touched his little body with my trembling hands. As my fingertips graced his face, I jumped back at the coldness of his skin.

"SAMMY!! SAMMY!! Oh no, no, no!!"

Making a mad dash to my room with tears cascading down my cheeks, I immediately grabbed my phone, dialed 911 and put the call on speaker. I could barely focus because my eyes were filled with warm liquid as my body shook uncontrollably.

"911 what is your emergency?"

"My baby isn't breathing, and his body is really cool!" I cried loudly as I rushed back to Sammy's crib and began administering CPR.

"Okay, what is your address ma'am?"

As I rattled off my address, she stated that the ambulance was on the way. "Ma'am the paramedics should be pulling up to your residence now! Can you let them in?" asked the operator.

Not wanting to leave Sammy by himself, I took drastic measures and lifted his tiny body out of the crib and ran to the front door. The ambulance and fire truck were pulling up just as I swung it open. One of the paramedics immediately jumped from the ambulance and ran to take the baby from my arms. He then shot to the rear of the ambulance as I followed behind screaming and crying.

"PLEASE SAVE MY BABY!!" I yelled. Tears were streaming from my eyes by the buckets.

At first, it looked as if they were fighting to save my little boy. Then the urgency slowed down. "WH–WH– WHAT ARE YOU DOING!!" I asked as the paramedic turned to me with tears in his eyes.

"I'm sorry," she said.

"SORRY?! NO, YOU HAVE TO SAVE MY BABY!!" I cried. "PLEEEEEEASE!!"

One of the other paramedics put his arm around me and tried to hold me. "I'm sorry ma'am. He was already gone when we arrived," he said.

"NO! NO!" YOU CAN SAVE HIM!!" I cried as I jumped in the back of the ambulance. "YOU HAVE ALL THIS EQUIPMENT! YOU CAN SAVE HIM!! Pleeeeaassssseee!!"

The sad and pitiful looks on their faces told me otherwise. I finally collapsed on the bench in the ambulance and scooped up my little boy. I cradled him in my arms as I cried harder than I've ever cried before. How could this have happened? How could my baby be dead? He had a machine to help him breathe... why did the doctor's take him off it so soon?! Why would they say he no longer needed it if this could possibly happen?!

After several minutes passed, the female paramedic finally spoke. "Ma'am, did your son have any health problems?"

Nodding my head, still hysterical, I explained that he had pneumonia not long ago. "Just last week he was removed from the breathing machines and was only on medication and breathing treatments!"

"Is there anyone that we can call for you?"

"I just want you to save my baby. Can you please try again?" I asked as I lifted my baby's cold body from the gurney and cradled him in my arms. I knew they couldn't save him. It was too late, but I was hoping for a miracle.

"I'm so sorry," the female paramedic apologized. "We're gonna take him to Texas Children's. Once the funeral arrangements are made, they'll be able to come and claim his body. We'll give you some time with him, but we're going to have to take him soon."

Ignoring the unacceptable words coming out of her mouth, I turned my attention to the beautiful baby I held in my arms. I couldn't believe that my precious baby was gone. I didn't want to leave him, but I didn't have a choice. However, I couldn't do this by myself.

Finally able to take a deep breath, I noticed that my phone was still clinched in my palm that was now drenched in sweat. Wiping it on my shirt, I thought about who I needed to call. The first person that came to mind was Tierra. Only after three times of dialing her up she still wasn't answering. Giving up, I knew who I had to call next...Smooth. Thankfully, he answered on the first ring.

"Hey, I was just about to head over there..."

"Please hurry!" I cried as I sat in the back of the ambulance cradling our now deceased son.

"What's wrong? Is something wrong with Sammy?" he asked with panic in his tone.

I didn't wanna tell him that our son died just yet. I didn't want him to get in an accident on the way. "Just hurry!" I said and ended the call.

My phone started to ring right back, and I thought it might be Smooth calling me back. But it wasn't. It was Tierra. I picked up right away as I still held onto my baby boy.

"Hey girl..."

"Tierra..." I called out as I busted out crying and handed the phone to the paramedic. She looked at me and I nodded my head for her to speak to Tierra.

"Hello ma'am, this is Lizzie Baines. I'm a paramedic with Fort Bend County. Can you please come over to your friend's house as soon as possible?" she asked. She paused. I guess Tierra was asking questions. "Something has happened, and your friend really needs you." Another pause. "Okay, I'll let her know."

She ended the call and handed the phone to me. The fire truck had backed out and left already. Exactly five minutes later, Smooth pulled up and jumped out of his truck. He almost fell to the ground trying to get to me. When he saw me holding Sammy in my arms, and the tears flowing from my eyes, he immediately started crying.

He slowly shook his head and brought his fist to his mouth to keep from crying out. "No, no, no, no!" he kept saying.

I nodded my head as tears continued to rain down my cheeks. He climbed into the back of the ambulance and sat next to me.

Reaching out for his son, I handed Sammy to him. He hugged him close and started bawling like a toddler, just like me. As the two of us were holding each other while cradling our baby, Tierra and Jay pulled up. One look at the scene in the rear of the ambulance caused them both to start crying. I kissed my baby on the forehead and exited the ambulance. I couldn't take it anymore and I needed my brother.

Releasing Sammy and Smooth, I jumped down out of the rear doors and ran into the arms of my brother and best friend. We all just started crying really hard while holding on to one another for dear life.

Tierra was smoothing my hair and telling me how sorry she was while Jay was stroking my back until Smooth hopped out of the ambulance. That man hit the ground so hard. I had never seen him cry like this before. I knew he had to be just as devastated as I was if not more.

Jay released me and went to help his friend. As I watched the emotional scene between the two homeboys, the paramedic interrupted to give me her card.

"If you need anything, please give us a call." She said then reminded me that they were going to bring the baby to Texas Children's.

My watery eyes stayed glued to her as she climbed in the ambulance and they drove away. My heart was broken right now. My baby was gone.

How can my baby be gone? Just yesterday, he was smiling and laughing. Now, he's dead?!

The realization of it caused me to start bawling hysterically. "Oh God! My baby is dead!!" I cried against Tierra's shoulder.

"I'm so sorry Tangi!" she said as she held me.

"What happened to him Tangi?" Smooth asked after several minutes. He still had tears in his eyes as he stared at me for answers. "What happened to my son?"

"I don't know. He was fine last night..."

"Did you forget to give him his breathing treatment?" Smooth asked as he ran his hands across his eyes.

"Wh-wh-what?" I asked. "No, I didn't forget!"

Is he trying to say this is my fault? Is he trying to blame our baby's death on me?

"Well what happened?" Smooth asked.

"I don't know! He was perfectly fine when I put him to bed last night. When I woke up this morning, I went straight to the nursery, but he wasn't breathing! That's how I found him... unresponsive and not breathing!" I cried.

"Did you give him the treatment this morning? What time did you give him his treatment?" Smooth rushed me with question after question and had me breaking down with guilt.

"Hold up now man. It sounds like you trying to put the blame on Tangi for Sammy's death," Jay said. "Y'all little boy was sick. It wasn't nobody's fault."

"You don't know that!" Smooth yelled towards Jay with tears and snot spewing. Then he turned his attention back to me. "What time did you give him his treatment this morning Tangi?!"

"I-I-I-I didn't. I didn't have a chance to! He was already gone by the time I woke up," I repeated in between sniffles.

"What time was that, huh?" Smooth asked.

"Almost 10, but..."

"YOU DID THIS!!" Smooth said as he pointed his finger in my face. "You should've woken up earlier..."

"Aye man, I know you feeling some kind of way because your baby died, but I'm not gonna stand here and let you put this on my sister. If you wanna keep shit real, you could've been here this morning to give the baby his treatment, but nooooo! Yo ass left and been staying in a hotel."

"What the fuck?" Smooth asked.

"It's true! This was neither your fault or hers! Blaming her isn't going to bring your boy back. You two need to pull together and be there for each other! Not lash out and blame each other for some shit that was beyond y'all control!" Jay suggested as he went and gave Smooth a brief hug and patted his back. "Y'all need to come together during this time."

My brother was right, I just prayed that Smooth was listening...

CHAPTER SEVENTEEN

Smooth

Devastated beyond belief, I couldn't stop myself from breaking down in front of everyone. I had never felt so much heartache and pain in my life! No parent should ever have to outlive their child, but there we were... Tangi and I had lost Sammy.

"I gotta go. I'll be back Tangi, but I gotta leave to get myself together."

"We'll stay here with you until Smooth comes back." Tierra assured her as she attempted to dry Tangi's endless tears.

"I don't wanna stay here right now. It's too painful to see all of Sammy's things knowing that he's never coming back!" she hollered out holding tightly onto Tierra.

Tangi's ear piercing screams sent chills up my spine and I was ready to get emotional again. It was all too much... just too fuckin' much.

Running off to my car before I broke down in tears again, I got in and went back to the hotel. When I got there, I locked myself in the room, came out of all my clothes and got in the shower. In there, I let it all out! I'm talking about crying in that muthafucka until the water turned cold. That was a long ass time for a hotel suite to run out of hot water!

Going from mad, to sad, to helpless, to trying to accept it all was confusing and frustrating. Jay was right though. I was thinking about how I needed to be there for Tangi through all this. After all, we were Sammy's parents. But after we buried Sammy, I was outta here. All the painful memories this town held was too much. I just wanted to start a new life somewhere else. Somewhere far away...

Trying to temporarily take my mind off Sammy's death, I turned on some upbeat music as I got dressed. My tears dried for a total of twenty minutes then they were right back flowing again.

Turning to my bag, I dug in the bottom and drew out the blunt I had stored in a green plastic vial. Going over to the window, I cracked it open as far as it went and lit that muthafucka up. I didn't stop puffing until the roach was burning my fingertips.

"Shit!" I moaned as I shook my hand like it was going to take the pain away.

As I walked to the bathroom to run my fingers under some cold water to get some relief, my cell rang. By the ringtone, I knew it was Tangi and I had to answer it.

There was no running from reality this time. I had to face it.

"Hey, I was just checking on you and letting you know that I didn't go to Jay's. I'm still at the house."

"I'm good," I lied holding back my emotions. "I'll be there in an hour or so."

That gave me time to go down to the old neighborhood church and get some praying in. That was the only way I could make some type of peace after my son was dealt a cold hand of death.

"Okay, I'll see you when you get here," Tangi sniffled before hanging up.

Grabbing my keys, I left the hotel and went to the chapel where I stayed on my knees for at least an hour. To some that may not be shit, but for a nigga like me who hadn't stepped foot in a church in over fifteen years, it was a big deal and I prayed that the good Lord above thought the same thing.

Coming out into the sunshine, I inhaled and exhaled a loud sigh of relief. I had actually been able to accept what happened and was ready to help make the final preparations for Sammy to be laid to rest.

As I drove to the house that I once shared with Tangi and Sammy, my high started kicking in. It had me relaxed until I reached my destination.

When I pulled up to Tangi's, my stomach got tied in knots, but I was able to suppress the tears. Swallowing deeply, I went and opened the screen door before letting myself inside.

"Hey," Tierra said standing up. "Tangi just got in the shower. We're gonna leave, but we'll be right around the corner at Jay's."

"Yeah, if you need anything, just holler man," Jay added as he patted my back and followed Tierra towards the front.

Easing behind, I walked them to the door, said my final goodbyes and then went back inside to find Tangi. I was worried about her.

"Tangi?" I called out through the locked bathroom door.

I called her a few more times before I used my fingernail to twist the middle of the knob and unlock it. Slowly entering the foggy room, I chanted her name twice more before I drew back the shower curtain and found her balled up at the bottom of the tub with scalding hot water hitting her body. Parts of her skin were burnt and bubbling while other sections were so raw that blood was leaking.

Immediately cutting the water off, I heaved Tangi into my arms and called the ambulance. I didn't know how to treat her wounds and wrapping her in a terry towel seemed more painful once the material stuck to her open wounds.

"Baby, why did you do this? Why would you do this to yourself?!" I cried trying to comfort her without hurting her as I dug in my pocket to get my cell. I had to call for help.

As I dialed 911 to get the paramedics sent over for the second time today, Tangi said nothing. She just stared off in space while blinking quickly to help her tears fall. She stayed that way until the medics came and took her to the hospital.

Waiting with her until they got her nice and sedated, I kissed her forehead then went to begin the funeral arrangements. I didn't want to do them without Tangi to help me, but in her condition, I didn't think she would be of any help. I couldn't afford to wait on her, and I didn't want my son lying in that cold ass morgue too long. I wanted Sammy to be resting in peace as soon as possible.

Going to the information desk at the hospital, I told them my situation and let them know where my son's body was being held. The older black man that worked behind the desk couldn't tell me shit, but he was able to point me in the direction of someone who could.

Traveling down the hall to the rear of the hospital, I found the office of Byron Hall. There he had all the pamphlets and information I needed to get started.

"Do you have someone who can help you? This is a difficult thing for a family to go through, so I couldn't imagine going through this alone," Mr. Hall questioned.

"Yeah, my son's uncle and I are pretty close. I'll call him once I leave," I told him with a heavy sigh. I was already beginning to feel overwhelmed with whether we should bury him or have him cremated.

"You have my deepest sympathy and condolences. The loss of a child, especially a baby is never easy. I pray that you find comfort in knowing that he's in the hands of the Lord now," Mr. Hall said.

That's easy for him to say. I hated when people said that shit. Like he was better off without his parents or something. He wasn't an unwanted baby and his parents loved him very much. So how was he better off without me or Tangi? How was he in a better place without his mother or father there to care for him? I didn't want to be rude and say the shit that I was thinking, so instead, I just didn't say shit. I just nodded my head and left his office.

It was apparent to me that he had never lost a child; otherwise, he wouldn't have come at me with that shit about being comforted. Nothing was going to comfort me. Nothing was going to take this pain away because my baby was dead. My baby was dead, and no one could tell me why he had to die.

With too many decisions to make on my own, I dialed Jay up. I told him all about what happened to Tangi after he left. He couldn't believe the shit, and neither could I. But she was grieving, and different people coped with death differently than others.

"She was in there doing that shit to herself when we were right in the other room?!" Jay gasped. "Where is she?"

"She's been admitted into the hospital, Memorial Hermann in Sugar Land. I think they might end up keeping her for a psych evaluation," I said.

"Bullshit! My sister isn't crazy, she's grieving! I mean, she just lost her baby boy!" he said. "Didn't you explain that shit to them?"

"She's not crazy Jay, but she did try to hurt herself. All this shit is happening while I'm still trying to wrap my head around the fact that my son is dead. That's why I was calling because I wanted to know if you and Tierra would help me make some decisions about his burial or memorial or whatever. Shit, I don't even know what to call it or what I wanna do. I got some papers from the hospital to show me what I need to take care of, but honestly man, I'm lost."

"Yea, we'll help you. I just need to go over to the hospital and see about my sister first. I'll give you a holla when I get back!"

"Okay, cool."

Hitting the power button on the stereo, I placed the satellite radio station on Shade 45 and bobbed my head to some new hip hop tune by Jay Z. It was my first time hearing it.

I stopped by the liquor store on my way back to the hotel. I purchased a bottle of Remy and hopped back in my truck. Getting lost in the lyrics of Jay Z's song, I made my way to my destination. I knew that I shouldn't be thinking about getting drunk, but what else could I do? I didn't want to go over to Tangi's place right now since it made no sense. I'd be there by myself surrounded by my son's things. I couldn't handle that shit, so I'd just wait in the hotel until Jay called me.

I got to the room and popped the top. I didn't even need a damn glass because I could drink it straight from the bottle. As I took a long swig of the warm liquid, it went down smoothly, but burned at the same time. It probably would've gone down better with ice, but fuck that! I wanted it to burn. This little burn that I was feeling in my chest was probably nothing like the burn my little boy felt in his lungs when he was fighting for air. I took another swig and then another. I didn't know how long it was going to take Jay to get back from the hospital. I just hoped I wasn't too fuckin' drunk to drive over to his place by the time he called.

A few drinks later, I heard my phone ringing. By that time, the liquor bottle was almost empty. I grabbed it off the bed and answered.

"Hello," I slurred.

"Aye man, whatchu doing? I've been calling you for the past half hour!" Jay said.

"I ain't doing nothing."

"Sound like you over there getting drunk as fuck!" he remarked.

"I ain't... I ain't... shit, I ain't drunk!" I lied.

"Yea, you are. Look man, put the bottle down and get some rest. We can go over the arrangements tomorrow when you're in a better frame of mind."

"I'm fine... I said I'm fine!"

"Yea, I know. But I gotta go by the club anyway, so get some rest and I'll see you tomorrow."

"Alright," I relented.

I really wasn't in any shape to do shit right now. My fuckin' head was spinning, and my heart was hurting. I hung the phone up and closed my eyes as thoughts of my son circled my brain until I fell asleep. I literally fell asleep with tears running from my eyes.

The next morning, I woke up and my head was still in a whirl. Struggling to find my way to the bathroom, I pissed and took care of my hygiene.

"UGH!" One look at myself in the mirror had me disgusted with myself. My son was gone and here I was getting drunk and shit instead of planning for his burial. What kind of father does shit like that? Before I could beat myself too much, I turned on the water to jump in the shower. Thank God the hot water was working again.

Closing the shower curtain after stepping in, I allowed the water to rain down on me as I started to cry again. What was I going to do without my baby boy? I had gotten so used to seeing him every day that I didn't know how I was going to be able to handle not having him around.

"Why God? Why would you take my boy from me? I would've given anything for my little boy to be able to live again. Why didn't you take me man?" I cried.

Knowing that I couldn't take my son's place no matter how much I begged, I washed my ass and stepped out. After I dried and dressed myself, I called Jay to see if we could meet up.

"Wassup buddy? How are you feeling?" he asked when he picked up.

"Well I'm sober..." I chuckled.

"That's good. You coming over?"

"Yea, is Tierra there?"

"Yea, she's here."

"Good. Since Tangi is still in the hospital, I'd like her help also."

"Yea, the doctors are going to keep Tangi for a few more days because of a couple of first-degree burns, but she should be released some time next week. So, as long as we do the burial next weekend, she should be able to attend," he explained.

"Good, I'm glad to hear it. If we could get these arrangements all done before she's released, that would be great," I said.

"Well, come on over bro. We're eager to help you."

"On my way."

I arrived at the house quicker than I anticipated still bumping Jay Z's new CD. Before I allowed myself to get wrapped up in my emotions again, I swallowed the lump in my throat and took my ass inside.

"Hey Smooth, how ya doin'?" Tierra asked with a low voice as she gave me a sympathetic hug and showed me in.

Escorting me to the den where Jay was sitting, I went in and took a seat on the recliner near the built-in gas fireplace. Looking up at me with bloodshot eyes, Jay reached out and pounded my fist before I handed him the pamphlets given to me by the dude at the hospital.

Tierra saw how lost we were and jumped right in and took over. She had everything taken care of by the time me and Jay had our third shot of whiskey.

Thank God she was there because if it would've been up to me and Jay, Sammy would've had a funeral and burial right here in their backyard. I know it sounded funny, but that was how much progress the two of us had made.

"Man, I don't know how you do that shit... holding up... being all strong and shit." Jay sighed heavily. "I don't have kids so I can't even imagine. All I know is this shit is killing me to see how it's tearing y'all up. Little man didn't deserve to be taken from us that way..."

Now this nigga had to get drunk to be starting this shit up again. Had us both sitting up there crying and Tierra joined us too. She took the bottle and started drinking straight from it.

"All the crazy shit that done happened in this past year... something good gotta come from it! This can't be it!" Tierra slurred as she began sobbing. "Tangi done did some fucked up shit in her life, but she never deserved no shit like this! Sammy didn't and you didn't either Smooth! This shit ain't fair!"

Getting up from her seat, Tierra grabbed her cell and began dialing. "Mom, how is Miracle?"

"See, she's been going crazy too!" Jay whispered as Tierra continued to talk loudly on the phone. "She can't concentrate long enough to watch Miracle, but it's killing her to be away from her."

"Mom, I know you just put her to sleep, but I need to see her... and no, I'm not drunk," she slurred then looked down at her screen. "Did she just hang up on me?"

"Baby, we can go get Miracle in the morning, but you're not about to go over there like this. We're both fucked up and yo mama ain't about to cuss me out," Jay laughed.

It was so good to have some true friends because I didn't know where I would be without Jay and Tierra during that emotional time. I was a mess and so was Tangi.

"I'm gonna go to stay with Tangi through this. I want her to be healthy enough to be there when we bury our son. It wouldn't be fair to do it without her," I told them as I stood to my feet and thanked them for everything they did. "I'll get that money for the services over to you today..."

"Smooth?! Are you serious?" Jay frowned. "I took care of all that. He was my nephew, my family and that makes you family. Don't worry about it. Just go help Tangi get better. That's all you need to do to repay me. That's all I ask."

What Jay was asking was understandable, but I didn't want him to get his hopes up. I didn't know how long I was going to be around after the memorial...

CHAPTER EIGHTEEN

Tierra

It broke my heart to see Smooth like that. Of course, I was worried about Tangi too, but to see a grown man break down like that really tugged at my toughest strings. I hated that they had to go through something like this, especially since Tangi had miscarried their first child before she had Sammy. I just knew when she got pregnant with this little boy that it was God's way of giving her a second chance at being a mother. Maybe she miscarried the first baby because he knew she wasn't ready. Who knew why she had that miscarriage? But in the wake of what happened yesterday, it didn't seem that important.

Oh, and Jay... he wasn't any better! He started crying and shit which made me cry too.

"Let's go to bed!" he suggested and grabbed me by my hand soon as Smooth left. "I need something to take my mind off all this sadness."

We both knew that reality would kick in as soon as our lovemaking session was over, but we didn't care. The temporary distraction was just what we needed!

After those thirty minutes of hip thrusting pleasure, we both were pooped. We couldn't even shower. We just laid there in our juices and passed out...

The next morning, I woke up in the bed alone. Jay was so old school that he left a written note on his empty side of the bed.

Good Morning Beautiful, I went to check on Tangi. I was gonna wait for you, but I knew you wanted to go see Miracle first. Call me when you wake up.

Setting the note on the bedside table with a smile, I got my cell out to call my mother first. Only I couldn't dial fast enough before there was an incoming call from a private number.

"Maybe this is Tangi," I thought aloud as I answered. "Hello?"

"Can you please come outside and talk to me? I've waited this long to get you alone..." Thaddeus belted out throwing me all the way off.

"I'm not at home..."

Beep, beep, beep!

"I know where you're at. I'm outside. You wanna come out or do you want me to kick that muthafucka's door in like I did yours?!" Thaddeus threatened.

Running to the front window, I kneeled on the white sectional and lifted the wooden blinds. "What the hell?"

I whispered in fear as I saw Thaddeus in his red Range Rover that was idling in front of Jay's house.

Beep, beep, beep!

My body jumped in fear as I tried to hang up and dial Jay while I failed miserably at setting the alarm. Good thing was, I put in so many wrong codes that it sent a silent alert to the security company and they would contact Jay. I just prayed that someone would come in time because Thaddeus had already killed the ignition and was getting out of the car.

"This nigga is seriously crazy?!"

BAM! BAM! BAM!

Now he was beating at the door. "TIERRA!" he called out loudly. "TIERRA OPEN THIS MUTHAFUCKA!!"

"GET OUTTA HERE THADDEUS!! I'M NOT IN THE MOOD TO FOOL WITH YOU AFTER WHAT YOU DID!!" I shouted back. "GO SEE SHEENA AND YOUR SON!!" I was trying my best to stall him out and I was hoping that it worked.

"Ain't nobody worrying about that fuckin' girl, and that ain't even my son!! Besides, she could never be you, baby! I need to see you. I miss you so much! You gotta tell me to my face that it's over!" he whined.

"IT'S OVER!!" I shouted.

"DAMMIT TIERRA... OPEN THE FUCKIN' DOOR!!" he shouted. Then his voice calmed down again. "I can't believe you would do this to me after everything we've been through together. Who was there for you when you were pregnant with Miracle? Huh? Me, that's who. Who took care of you after you had that C-section? Me! I went through that whole pregnancy with you! I took care of Miracle too and I didn't mind because I love her like she's my own! I deserve to be in her life! You can't just push me out Tierra!"

Where the fuck is the help that I need? This muthafucka is psycho!

My cell started ringing and when I checked to see who it was, I saw that it was Jay calling. I wanted to answer him but was afraid to hang up on Thaddeus. When I didn't answer my cell, the house phone began to ring. I rushed over to pick it up!

"Hello!"

"Tierra what's going on? The alarm company just called me and said that the alarm code was being entered in wrong."

"Jay, Thaddeus is here..."

"What the fuck? I know you ain't telling me that nigga is outside... on my fuckin' property!!"

"TIERRA!! OPEN THIS FUCKIN' DOOR BABY OR I'M ABOUT TO BUST THROUGH THAT MUTHAFUCKA IN FIVE, FOUR..."

"Jay hurry please!" I cried. "I don't know what he'll do if he gets in!"

"Baby listen, I'm still a few minutes away. I want you to go to the bedroom and look under the bed. There's a locked box under there with a gun inside..."

"I can't shoot a gun!" I cried.

BANG! BANG!

"Oh my God! He's trying to break the door!"

"Go get the box! The key for the box is in the top drawer of the nightstand on the left side! Hang up and call the police!!" he ordered.

"Okay, okay..."

"NOW TIERRA!!" Jay shouted.

BANG! BANG!

While Thaddeus was still trying to get in, I hung both phones up. Then I went to get the locked box as I dialed 911.

"911 what is your emergency?"

"Someone is breaking down my front door!" I cried as I pulled out the locked box. I pulled the drawer open and tried to find the key.

"TIERRA!!"

BOOM! BOOM! BOOM!

I heard the door split open as I found the key.

"Ma'am I need your address!"

I rattled off Jay's address as I unlocked the box. I could hear Thaddeus inside the house. "Please help me," I whispered as I quietly made my way to the closet. "I have a gun, but I don't wanna use it."

"Police are on the way ma'am. Just try to be as quiet as possible. I'll stay on the line with you until the police get there," the operator said.

"TIERRA WHERE THE FUCK YOU AT BITCH?!!" he yelled as he found his way to the bedroom.

I tried not to make any noises as he made his way to the bathroom to check for me. "I JUST WANTED TO LOVE YOU, BUT NOW, I'M GONNA FUCK YOU UP... AFTER I GET SOME OF THAT GOOD PUSSY!!" he continued.

I heard him come out of the bathroom and he was heading to the closet. I prayed the police got here soon.

"Tierra I'm coming to get you baby," he said.

As the doorknob turned a little, my heart literally dropped to my stomach. I held my breath until I heard Thaddeus holler in pain.

"Nigga you got me fucked up if you thought you was gon' break in my fuckin' house!"

Oh, thank God! Jay was here. I was afraid to move as I heard the two of them fighting it out in the bedroom. "Ma'am what's going on?" asked the operator.

"My boyfriend just got home and they're fighting! Where the hell is the police?" I asked.

"They should be arriving very shortly ma'am!"

"I-I-I have to go see what's going on!"

"No ma'am, you need to stay put until the police arrive!"

"That's my man out there with some crazy person! I'm not just gonna sit in here and wait for the police! What if he's getting beaten up? I have to make sure he's alright!" I said.

I couldn't believe this shit was happening. Why didn't these niggas show us how crazy they were before we started fucking them? UGH!

Slowly making my way to the closet door, I heard the police sirens in the near distance. It sounded like someone was getting their ass beat for sure, but I was scared to come out.

As I heard the police cars pull into the driveway, the closet door opened. I sat on the floor and held the gun up until Jay's face came into view. I breathed a sigh of relief as he reached for me. Dropping the gun on the floor, I took his hand as he pulled me into a tight hug.

"Who were you supposed to shoot with that gun?" he asked as he chuckled.

"I was gonna shoot his ass if he had opened that door... right between the eyes!" I laughed with tears flowing.

"Babe, you weren't gonna shoot shit with the safety off. You didn't even cock the hammer."

We heard a bunch of footsteps making their way in and saw police with their guns drawn. We raised our hands immediately. There was no way I was about to get my ass shot up in here...

CHAPTER NINETEEN

Thaddeus

I had been miserable without Tierra the past couple of weeks. She wasn't accepting my phone calls and wasn't responding to any of my text messages. I tried to move on and forget about her, but I couldn't. I just loved her and missed her so much. I didn't understand how she could just screw me over like that for that nobody. What the fuck did he have that I didn't?

I made my way to her house that morning after finishing the bottle of Seagram's Gin. When I got to her house, she wasn't there. I knew where she was though, so I headed to that nigga's place. When I saw him leave, I thought that was my chance to speak to her. I called her hoping that she'd open the door and have a conversation with me like normal people, but I should've known better.

After begging her to come out and talk to me, she wouldn't. Of course, that meant I had to let myself in. In the midst of breaking down that fucking door, I hurt my damn shoulder. I finally made my way in and started hunting her down.

Why the hell did this nigga have to have so many fucking bedrooms? He only got one ass and no kids!

Huffing as I spotted a set of double doors at the end of the hallway, I knew it had to be the master. On my way there, I stopped and checked all the showers and closets before I crept into the bedroom. Lightly stepping to the other side of the bed in front of the closet, I saw the unlocked gun box on the floor. I wasn't worried though because I knew Tierra hated guns. She wouldn't be able to shoot a gun if Yosemite Sam had taught her ass.

As I was about to open the closet door assuming that she would be in there, I felt a hard knock on the back of my head. Next thing I know, me and that nigga was duking it out. I didn't know what his intentions were for me, but I was trying to kill that muthafucka. However, considering I was quite a bit drunk it wasn't long before he started to get the best of me.

As he punched me over and over again, I could feel myself slipping into unconsciousness. As my head began to spin, I heard sirens coming closer. I wanted to run, but I couldn't do it with somebody else's legs at this point.

That nigga was letting me have it and didn't stop until he heard footsteps enter his place. He then opened the closet door and there was my baby. More than anything I wanted to punch the shit out of him for putting his hands all over her like that, but when the cops arrived, I found myself being handcuffed for breaking and entering.

Ain't that some shit! I got my ass beat up, lost my woman, and now I'm facing charges! What the fuck did I do to deserve this when all I wanted was to love that woman?

Barely able to see out of my right eye, I watched the two of them holding each other lovingly as they spoke to police. That shit made me sick to my stomach, so as I was being led out of the room, I stopped the officer and opened my mouth. *Yea, I did it.*

I vomited all over that beautiful thick and plush carpeting in their master bedroom. I didn't stop until I had emptied everything I had consumed from last night and this morning. I smiled through my black eyes and swollen lips as I glanced back at them.

Serves them right for doing me the way that they did...

When we got to the precinct, I was booked and released. Heading out the security gate with my clear plastic bag containing my belongings, I saw that I had my cell but not my wallet. I must have left it in my car which was parked across the street from that nigga Jay's crib. Since I was served with an order of protection to stay away from Tierra and his address was on the paper, it was going to be hard to go get that muthafucka.

Only person that I could call that I knew would come was Sheena. After I got her on the line and told her my version of the story, she forgot all about the fighting we had been doing and came right down to get me.

Waiting outside of the precinct, I paced back and forth for about ten minutes. That was how long it took Sheena to get here.

"What the hell happened to you?" she shrieked when I got in her car. My face was fucked up, so I had to come up with a good one.

"I told you they jumped me baby. I told Tierra that I was gonna take this test and prove to her that you had my son," I continued to make up some far-fetched story that Sheena bought right into. "I'm gonna drop you at the corner of the house. I need you to take me by there and drive my car and I'll drive yours."

Smiling proudly, she zoomed me on Jay's block, walked to my ride then met me at my place. When we got there, we went inside, and Sheena began waiting on me hand and foot. That was just what I needed.

After she took care of my every need, and I do mean EVERY... I got her good and comfortable then had her go get her son. Since I had got the home paternity test in the mail that I ordered, I was going to sneak and swab the boy.

Getting everything prepared while she was away, I began drinking. Of course, I had already swabbed my mouth. I didn't want the alcohol to fuck up the test. I had to get fucked up to pretend that this little boy was mine when I had a good feeling that he wasn't. I mean sure, there was a slim chance the kid belonged to me, but I wasn't claiming shit until the test results came back.

Ding, dong...

Answering the door, I let Sheena and her son in. This time I got the chance to take a good look at him. "He's a handsome lil' fella," I said as I laughed and as he ran up to me and hugged me. She even had him calling me 'daddy'! I wanted to chin check that ho' for pulling that shit, but I reminded myself that I needed to get that test done before I did something else crazy.

My reckless decisions and actions had gotten me in a whirl of trouble the past month. I lost my fiancée, I had gotten my ass beat a few times then to top shit off, I got thrown in jail for trying to get my woman back.

Now look at me! Stuck over here playing daddy to a bitch I know that I don't wanna be with!

Continuing the charade, I kicked it with Sheena and her son until they both passed out in my bed early that evening. Rushing to the bathroom cabinet, I got the kit out to swab the little boy. He was lightly snoring, and I had to gently pry his lips apart to swab him.

Placing the sample in the appropriate sterile envelope, I put it away until the morning. Then I could drop the sealed packages at the clinic down the street. That way I would only have to wait two days for the results.

Boy, that was the longest night of my life, but when I handed the woman behind the counter those samples, I sighed in relief. I was finally going to get some answers.

On the way out the door, my brother Hakim called and checked on me. I hadn't been down to the gym in a few days and had lied to him and told him that I hadn't been feeling well.

"You straight bruh?"

"Yeah, I'm feeling better. I'm just out picking up some meds," I said shaking my head at the person I was becoming. It was ugly, but I couldn't control it. I couldn't control shit that was why my life. My life was falling apart right in front of my eyes.

"I just heard about Tierra's friend Tangi losing her son..."

"What?" I said remembering that Tierra had mentioned something like that while we were arguing last. I was so drunk I forgot all about her saying that shit.

"Yeah, apparently he stopped breathing in his sleep and the mother found him unresponsive in his crib. Tierra didn't tell you?"

"Yeah, but I've been so ill that I've been at my place the last few days. I didn't want to get her or Miracle sick."

"Well, you better get well and go check on her. I'm sure she needs you, bro. That shit has got to be hard on her. Didn't you say that the little boy was her godson?" Hakim asked.

"Yea. Damn! That shit must be killing her and Tangi," I said.

"I'm sure it is. You need to go see her man."

"I will, as soon as I'm better," I said before hanging up.

My heart went out to Tierra. I knew she was fucked up behind that shit and there I was making things worse for her. I had to do something to get back into her life, even if it meant putting Jay out the picture for good...

All the way back to my place, I was thinking of a plan to get Tierra to stop fucking with Jay. I could get him locked up, but that was some bitch shit. Jail was no place for a black man.

"Maybe I can dig up some dirt on him. He has to be involved in something illegal to have that bad ass crib and own that upscale nightclub," I thought aloud as I contemplated my next move.

I had to make my next move my best one...

CHAPTER TWENTY

Tangi

Laying up in that hospital bed all alone was scary as hell. There was no Smooth, no Tierra, no Jay and worst of all, no Sammy.

The meds the doctor put me on had me so groggy and disorientated that I couldn't force another tear out if I wanted to. It was like my whole body was floating and I was laying there watching it. Well, I did for as long as I could keep my eyes open.

For the next two days, I was in and out of consciousness and barely remembered what was going on. I recalled seeing Tierra for a minute and a glimpse of Jay another time, but mainly I kept having flashes of Smooth being there with me. He was always holding my hand and talking to me. I didn't know what he was saying, but just the sound of his voice soothed me.

On the third day, the doctors began weaning me off the meds and I started feeling the pain of my wounds. I also couldn't stop thinking about the morning I found Sammy in his crib.

"Hey baby," Smooth greeted me that day with a kiss to my cheek as he came into my hospital room and sat beside me. "You ready to have this meeting and talk about what happened?"

"Yes, only because I'm ready to get out of here. My wounds are healing, and I know what I tried to do to myself was wrong," I hurried up and confessed.

"You'll be out by tomorrow and we'll be able to lay our son to rest..."

"And after that?" I asked sadly as I looked up at him.

"Let's just take it one day at a time. First, let's have this session and then let's get you home..."

"I don't think I can go there with all Sammy's things still there. That place holds too many memories. I don't think I ever want to go back there."

As Smooth clinched my palm tightly, he spoke to me calmly. "I will go tonight and get everything packed up until you can decide what you want to do."

"Well where am I gonna go when I get out?"

"You can either go to your brother's house or stay with me at the hotel. I just don't want you to be alone."

Knowing I didn't want to be anywhere but with him, I told him that I was going to the hotel with him. I loved my brother and Tierra, but no one could understand what Smooth and I were going through as parents. It was our worst nightmare.

"Okay, are you two ready?" The nurse came in and asked before whisking us off to a conference room on the second floor of the hospital.

I didn't know what to expect when we got in there, but once we started talking everything just began to flow out. Smooth and I both were able to get a lot of stuff off our chest.

"Thank you for being here for me," I said to Smooth once we got back into my room.

"This is where I'm supposed to be. Sammy was our son and we should go through this together," he sighed as he stood up. "I'm gonna go and get this packing done. I'm gonna have to hire someone to help me with all that shit."

I understood exactly where Smooth was coming from, he was tired both mentally and physically and I felt the same way. I hated that I was stuck in the hospital and I couldn't help him like I wanted to. My dumb ass had to go and hurt myself. Now that I looked back at what I did, I knew that I was losing it. I was thankful that it wasn't much worse.

"Well call me when you get settled. I just wanna hear your voice before I go to sleep."

"I gotcha baby," he promised with a kiss to seal the deal. That was enough for me to doze off comfortably soon as he left my room. I was in a deep sleep too, but

Tierra popped up a few hours later and woke me up. She had to fill me in on everything that happened with Thaddeus. I couldn't believe what she was telling me, and I wouldn't have either if I wouldn't have seen her wounds to prove it.

"Wow, and I thought he was the perfect man!" I gasped in disbelief.

"You and me both boo!" Tierra laughed. "I got an order of protection against him now, so hopefully he'll get the picture and stay the hell away."

No sooner than the words left her mouth, Thaddeus was ringing her cell. Tierra's face frowned up so hard that her forehead wrinkled. She was cussing before she even connected the call.

"I knew I should've blocked this muthafucka!" she hissed. "What the hell..."

"I just wanted to check on you. I heard about what happened to Tangi's son." I could hear him since the room was in total silence.

"Look, we are all okay and we will remain that way if you stay the hell out of all of our lives Thaddeus! I'm so done with you after you put your fucking hands on me!"

"Wait!" I could hear him holler out. "I went and got that paternity test! I'll have the results in a few days! Just wait and see Tierra, that's not my son."

"I could give a rat's ass if that's your son or not! Miracle is my daughter and that's the only child I'm thinking about right now besides my godson who we have to lay to rest soon! So right now, you're causing nothing but more anguish by harassing me!"

"I will give you these few days Tierra, but after you help bury your godson, we are gonna talk."

"Why can't you just accept that it's over and move on Thaddeus?"

"Because I love you and Miracle, and I don't wanna be without you two. You're my family! Just remember what I said Tierra. Three days!"

Suddenly Tierra's face went blank. She said Thaddeus had hung up on her. Quickly pushing a bunch of buttons on her cell, she put his number on block.

"You know he can call you from another phone right?" I laughed knowing the shit wasn't funny, but my meds had me feeling giddy at the moment.

"And I'll block the next one and the next one after that until that fool gets the message. I'm so damn sick of his ass! I wish he would just get the hell out of my life!" Tierra fussed then looked at me. "Let me stop bothering you with all my drama when you're going through such a hard time yourself. I'm so sorry for being insensitive Tangi."

"It's quite alright and actually it took my mind off everything for a bit." I giggled. "You got anything else juicy to share. Like something about you and my brother and how you two are bumping pelvises?"

"See, there you go Tangi!" she smirked playfully. "We are just friends who happen to enjoy each other's company."

"Nah, you two are fucking and falling in love. Don't deny it because it's a beautiful thing, not to mention that shit is rare. Not too often do you find a man that can take care of you and you enjoy being around. Like a homie and a lover that you can trust."

"Girl, I'm just mad I waited so long to give Jay some play. Just think if I would've fucked with him back in the day instead of getting mixed up with the likes of Dallas..." Tierra pursed her lips and looked up in the air.

"It happened now for a reason. You both are more mature and have been through so much shit that you can now appreciate one another." I guessed, not knowing what the hell I was saying. The second dose of meds was the sleepy ones and I was dozing off on Tierra.

"Girl, I see you're tired, so I'm gonna get out of your hair and let you rest. I just had to come down here and check on you since we haven't had a chance to chat since all this craziness began," Tierra said as she rose from the chair. "Just know that I love you and I'm keeping you in my prayers. I'm just a phone call away and I'll be here if you call boo."

"Thanks Tierra. You're the best girl," I whispered before my eyes fully closed.

That night I dreamt about burying Sammy. Just the vision of his tiny body in a casket made me shake in my sleep. I didn't know if I could bear seeing him like that. I was already traumatized by being the one to find him lifeless and no matter how hard I tried, I couldn't get that picture out of my head.

Waking up in a sweat after only a couple of hours of sleep, I called for the nurse. I needed someone to be in the room with me before I drove myself crazy.

"Are you okay?" she asked as she turned off the 'call' button.

"No, I can't sleep, and my mind is all over the place." I confessed feeling confused on what to do with myself.

"Is there someone I can call for you?" she offered as she gave me something to help relax me.

Instead of answering her question, I just thanked her and waited for her to leave the room so I could call Smooth. I hated to bother him when he had so much other shit to do, but I needed him.

"You okay?" he answered like he was out of breath.

"No, I'm just going through it and wanted to talk to you."

"I'm just finishing up at the house. I'll be right up there."

Smooth came up there that night and climbed right in bed with me. He stayed with me the entire night, holding me close to him. It felt so good being in his arms, even if we were in this small hospital bed. I thought that he didn't care about me anymore, but now it looked like I thought wrong.

The nurse woke us up a couple of times during the night to check my vitals. She didn't tell him to get out of the bed, so he didn't. He stayed with me holding me until I got released the next morning. Now it was time to prepare myself to get through Sammy's memorial.

I don't know how I'm gonna do it...

CHAPTER TWENTY-ONE

Smooth

It was hard as hell to stay by Tangi's side when I couldn't stop blaming her for what happened. It was even harder to look at myself in the mirror. I was just as much at fault as she was. I should've been there. I knew the meds that the doctor prescribed her for that fucking postpartum depression shit made her sleep hard!

I should've been there. Why wasn't I there?!

Temporarily pushing all the guilt to the side, I made the final preparations for Sammy. Tierra and Jay had gone all out by getting doves and carriages and a bunch of other flashy shit. I didn't see the point, but I didn't say shit. I just appreciated the help because I definitely couldn't have done it by myself.

"Baby, what time is the car picking us up tomorrow?" Tangi asked as she walked around the hotel suite still looking lost.

"Well, the service starts at ten, so I think they'll be scooping us up around nine. We also have to swing by and pick up Tierra and Jay before we head to the church."

Tangi walked over to me and wrapped her arms around my waist. "Thank you for being here for me," she said as she held me tightly with her face pressed against my chest.

"You don't have to thank me Tangi. To be honest, I needed you just as much as you needed me. Sammy was our son, so we needed to be there for each other," I admitted.

If only I could stop blaming her for what happened, we could probably get our relationship back on track. I tried to do that, but I couldn't. Just because I wasn't voicing those feelings to her didn't mean they were forgotten about. I just didn't want to make her feel worse than she was already feeling. Hell, if she was feeling half as bad as I was then she was in bad shape because my head was still fucked up.

Why my son though?!

Sammy was just getting started. He was only four months old. I still had trouble processing the fact that my son was gone. Knowing that I wasn't going to be able to see his handsome little face anymore had me broken up inside.

"I'm really sorry for everything I put you through Sam. I wish I could take it all back and be honest with you, but I can't. I know you said that you need to take it one day at a time, but I really wanna be with you. I couldn't get through this without you. I don't know what I'm going to do if you decide not to take me back," she confessed.

Gripping her hand, I pulled her to sit with me on the bed. "Look Tangi, I'm not insensitive to what you're going through because I lost a son too. I just don't think we can be together at this point..."

"Because I lied..."

"That's a big part of it. I mean, you should've told me the truth about everything from day one. You kept things a secret from me for whatever reason. I thought you knew how much I loved you and wanted to be with you..."

"I do know!"

I shook my head no. She couldn't have known how much I cared because if she did, she wouldn't have hidden so much pertinent shit from me. Of course, I wouldn't have been happy to know that she was fucking around with her best friend's husband, but at least I would've known the truth before I was all in love and shit. She should've divulged that info, so I could've decided if I wanted to continue seeing her or not. Chances are that I would've run from her though. That was some foul shit.

Then to top it off, she had me believing she was pregnant with my kid the first time. I was super happy that she was carrying my seed. Then when she miscarried, I was devastated. She didn't seem too deeply affected by the loss though, but I never questioned it. I mean, different people deal with shit in different ways. So, when I found out that she was carrying Dallas' seed and that she had terminated the pregnancy herself by taking that shit, I understood why she wasn't as emotional about the miscarriage as I was.

The fact that she lied to me and kept that shit a secret for over a year stung like a muthafucka. Had I known the kid was Dallas', I don't know how I would've reacted because clearly, she was fucking both of us during the same time frame at one point.

"Obviously you didn't because you would've known that you could tell me anything and as long as you were being truthful, I'd still love you."

"I didn't mean to lie Sam. It just seemed easier not to say anything than to tell you I was pregnant with Dallas' child. I didn't want to hurt you," she said.

"But how do you think I feel now Tangi? I'm devastated that we loss Sammy. I blame you for not checking on him soon enough, but I blame myself as well. I should've been there, and if it wasn't for your lies and deceit, I would've been."

Tears streamed down her face as she looked away from me. I knew that I was hurting her, and I didn't mean to, but I had to be honest with her. There was no sense in keeping the truth from her to spare her any pain. I knew that we were going through something that no parent should ever have to face. Tomorrow we had to bury our precious little boy. No parent should ever have to go through no shit like that. A child is supposed to bury their parents because we've been around longer. Not the other way around.

"I know I fucked up. I can't explain to you how sorry I am, but I am. I just need you to forgive me so we can move on. I don't know how to do this without you. I don't wanna do this without you," she said as she leaned against me and started bawling again.

The last thing I wanted to do was make love to Tangi as a way to cope with our grief. But the way I was feeling right now, I needed her in a different kind of way. I knew that I shouldn't go there, but I had to.

Lifting her face with my finger on her chin, she looked up into my eyes as I brought my lips to hers. She responded the way I expected her to as she opened her mouth to receive my tongue. As my hands roamed her body, we laid next to each other in the bed on top of the covers. When I lifted her shirt, she didn't stop me. I tossed it to the side and removed her bra, releasing her plump breasts. Bringing my mouth to her erect nipples, Tangi held on to the back of my head to guide me. Instantly she began releasing moans of satisfaction as my tongue circled rings around her areolas. Slipping my hand inside her shorts, I began to gently finger her.

"Mmmmmm," she hummed softly as she opened her legs wider. I felt her body shiver at the time my fingers became sticky with her juices.

Removing my fingers, I stood up and quickly removed my clothing while Tangi took her bottoms off and threw them on the floor. I climbed back in the bed on top of her where my erect member found comfort between her warm folds.

"Mmmmmm," she moaned as she grabbed my face and stuffed her tongue in my mouth. I kissed her hungrily as I thrust hard and powerful inside of her. "Oh shit!"

Staying silent, I kept banging her into oblivion. Her body shuddered beneath me as she released her juices onto my pole. "I want it from the back," she requested.

Shit! She didn't have to ask me twice. I withdrew my stiff rod as Tangi quickly got on her hands and knees, face down, ass all the way up. Her back was arched just the way I liked it as I got behind her and slammed my pipe into her backside.

"Oh God!" she cried out as I began to pump hard and fast.

"Aw shit!" I groaned as I felt my nut building.

Continuing to go hard and deep inside her, I couldn't keep my orgasm back any longer. I gripped her hips and pressed me body against her ass while I quaked like crazy. My knees were shaking and everything. My nut was on overload as it exploded inside her. Her body trembled as she cried out and released her own honey.

We collapsed beside each other breathing hard and sweating profusely. "Whewwww!" she exclaimed.

I just kept taking deep breaths in and blowing them out. I hadn't intended for this to happen, but it did, and I had no regrets. She cuddled up next to me and draped her arm across my torso.

"No matter what happens between us, I want you to know that I'll always love you Sam. You have always treated me like a queen, and I appreciate that. Until you came into my life, I never knew how I was supposed to be loved. That's why it was easy to fall into a relationship with Dallas. I recognize that what I did was wrong, and I should've never gone there with him. However, if I hadn't been with him first, I wouldn't have known how to appreciate you. You are a wonderful man and I really wish I had done some things, a lot of things, differently. I just hope that one day, you'll be able to forgive me," Tangi apologized from the heart and I felt that shit.

"I love you too Tangi. I've never been in love with any woman the way I've loved you. I just don't know if love is enough to keep us together. So much has happened between us. I just need some time to think this shit through," I said. I decided that now was a good time to let her know about my plans to leave town. If anyone should understand, it should be her. After all, she ran away at one point herself. Shit, I still didn't know where she was.

"How much time?"

"I don't know," I said as I took a deep breath. "I think you should know that I'm leaving tomorrow."

"You're leaving? What do you mean by that?"

"I can't stay here Tangi. This city holds too many memories for me. I can't function here," I said.

"But where are you going?"

"I'd prefer not to say right now."

"But I don't want you to go..."

"I didn't want you to leave either that time, but you did. And when you came back, you were in a much better space than when you left. I need to do this for me. I'm no good to anyone as long as I stay here in Houston. I have to go..."

"But what about us?"

"I told you that I need time!"

"When are you leaving?" she asked through tears.

"Right after the services."

"Will I ever see you again?"

"Maybe... I don't know..."

"Maybe?! Please stay! Don't leave me!" she cried.

Climbing on top of me, Tangi started kissing me hard and passionately.

"I don't want you to go," she panted. She slipped my swollen dick inside her again and started bouncing on it. This wasn't the answer because at the end of the day, I was still gonna leave... but it sure felt good.

As we ravaged each other's bodies for the next hour or so, I enjoyed it. I didn't know when I'd be able to get involved with another woman, so I was going to enjoy the pussy that I was getting now.

By the time we were done, all we could do was collapse in bed and fall asleep. I was glad because I didn't want to discuss anything else. Tomorrow was going to be difficult enough, so I just wanted to sleep right now.

Tomorrow was gonna be hard as fuck...

CHAPTER TWENTY-TWO

Tierra

Messing around with Jay, I woke up this morning with a swollen vagina. I wasn't complaining because I loved every moment that I spent with him.

Rolling out of his arms with a heavy heart, I thought about Sammy as I got ready. Having to bury Tangi's baby today was going to be one of the hardest things we've ever had to face. I knew how much she loved her little boy. She was completely devastated and so was Smooth. Even Jay was torn up. He had barely been eating or sleeping and continuously spoke of his nephew and the struggles he had gone through with his health. Even though Tangi's baby had struggled with his breathing since his bout with pneumonia, we never expected this to happen.

When Sammy was alive, sometimes I found myself feeling a little guilty that my baby girl was perfect, and Sammy had so many problems. He was such a tiny little thing and didn't deserve none of the stuff that had happened to him. Tangi stated a couple of times that it must be her karma for all that she had done to me in the past. I quickly brushed it off and assured her that wasn't the case.

Now that I was thinking about it, maybe that was her karma. I mean, nothing good had happened to her since I found out about her and Dallas. I felt so sorry for her.

As I searched the closet for my heels, I glanced at my watch. It was almost 9:20 so I knew that Tangi and Smooth would be here soon to pick up me and Jay. I knew I might have gone a little overboard with the preparations for the service for Sammy, but I just wanted him to have the best homegoing ever.

"You almost ready?" Jay asked as he kissed my neck while he stood behind me.

"Yea. Let me just put my earrings on and I'll be good to go."

"Good, because Smooth texted and said they were down the street."

"I'll be done by the time they get here."

Fetching the diamond set that Jay had recently given me, I stood in the mirror to put them on. A couple of minutes later, I heard a horn honking in the driveway.

"Tierra let's go!" Jay called from the front room.

Snatching my purse off the bed, I headed toward the front door. Jay locked up and followed behind me. As we walked to the car, I heard a beep from my phone. I didn't bother to check it because whoever it was wasn't as important as what was going on right now.

Clearing his throat to gain my attention, Jay opened the door and I slid into the seat. First thing I did when I saw Tangi's sad face was reach out and give her a warm hug. "How are you holding up?" I asked.

"I don't know if I can do this Tierra," she said as tears slid from her eyes. "I have to bury my baby today. How can I possibly do that?"

"You'll get through it. You have all of us to support you too. I know it's gonna be hard Tangi, but you are such a strong person."

I was trying to make her feel good about herself. Yes, their baby was dead, but that didn't mean she had to be dead too. This was going to be hard for Tangi to get past, but eventually, she would get where she needed to be. Then who knows... maybe she would have the chance to have another baby somewhere down the road.

Catching my attention, I spotted Smooth and Jay huddled up on the opposite of us whispering. I immediately wondered what they were talking about. I didn't want to pry, so I let them have their moment. I was sure that Smooth was feeling just as horrible as Tangi. He was in need of comforting as well, so I was glad that Jay could be there for him.

"Smooth is leaving," Tangi whispered.

"What? Where's he going?" I asked.

"I don't know. He won't tell me, but he said he's leaving right after the funeral because there are too many memories here."

"What the hell kind of shit is that? The two of you need each other!" Tierra whispered back.

"I know. I told him that I love him and don't want him to leave, but he said he has to go."

Tears began to stream from her eyes. She dabbed at them and sniffled. "Uuuuuhhhh!" I was about to say something to Smooth before Tangi bumped my knee with hers.

Shit, she knew how I was. If she didn't want me to ask him nothing, she shouldn't have told me nothing.

"You alright babe?" Jay asked.

"Yea, I'm fine."

Shortly after, we pulled up to the church. The four of us filed out of the vehicle and braced ourselves as we headed inside. My eyes widened as I saw that there was standing room only. Thankfully they had the front bench reserved for us.

Drawing back the gold ribbon, I ushered everyone onto the pew, positioning myself between Tangi and Jay. As I got as comfortable as possible considering the sad occasion, I eyed the sanctuary to see all the strangers.

Out of all the family Tangi had, I only knew a few of them.

You shall cross the barren desert, but you shall not die of thirst...

The music began as the lead singer of the choir belted out the first verse of, 'Be Not Afraid'. The notes she hit with precision sent chills up my spine and tears down my cheeks.

If anything could break you down at a funeral, it was a good old fashion hymn sung by a woman with that southern church voice. It would do it every time! There wasn't a dry eye in the place when the music ceased, and the pastor got up and began speaking.

The service was really short and after 20 minutes in, he was wrapping it up. That was just how Smooth wanted it... quick, fast, and sweet.

"At the parent's request, we're not gonna ask folks to come up and share. Instead, Samuel will come up and say a few words before we have the viewing."

Smooth bent over and kissed Tangi's lips before sliding out of the pew and taking his place behind the podium. My heartrate sped up in anticipation of what he had to say. Scooting over a bit, I held onto Tangi and comforted her as he spoke.

"I just wanna thank everyone for coming and supporting us during this difficult time. Tangi and I wouldn't be about to make it through without it..." Smooth closed his eyes and paused before he continued. "Weeping may endure for a night, but joy cometh in the morning... the last time I heard that scripture from the book of Psalm, we were laying my grandmother to rest. I was just a small boy and didn't quite understand what it meant then, but now I think I get it. Let us shed our final tears today, but once we're done, let us rejoice in life. We have to live on in order for Sammy's spirit to live on within us. Our little boy may not have lived a long life, but the time he was around had a huge impact on those closest to him. He was such a fighter. Even though he was ill, that never stopped him from smiling at me or his mother. I'm really gonna miss my son. Sammy, I'm trying to push through, but it's hard. Know that your mother and I love you very much. Rest easy son."

As Smooth eased back from the podium to return to the pew, the music began playing again. He sat on the end and held Tangi close. Despite what Tangi said about Smooth leaving, I felt that they would be alright as a couple. Grief had a way of bringing people closer together. I was confident from what I was seeing that Smooth wouldn't be able to leave Tangi behind no matter what he said.

Row by row beginning with the rear, folks lined up to view the body on the way out. We were last and thank goodness because Tangi fell over Sammy's casket screaming and crying. Smooth rushed to lift her into his arms as Jay held on to me. The whole scene had me hysterical. I couldn't stop crying as I glanced from Tangi throwing a fit to her little baby boy lying in that casket dressed in an all-white suit. His little face was bloated, but lil' Sammy was still as handsome as ever.

"Come on baby," Smooth urged while escorting Tangi back to the limo. "It's almost over. Just another hour or so, we will be at your brother's surrounded by all your family."

Smooth wasn't lying either! We went to cemetery and made it back to Jay's before one.

"Dang, look at all these cars!" I gasped as I saw people parking, getting out and going up to the door.

"My uncle Lewis is there with the caterers, so he'll let everyone in," Jay said as the limo pulled us right up to the door.

Everyone rushed both Jay and Tangi soon as we got in the door. It was so overwhelming that after an hour of all that talking over the old school music that they were playing I needed a break.

Since there were folks in damn near every room of Jay's house and in the backyard, I had to take my cell out front to call my mother. I wanted to check on Miracle.

"She's fine Tierra. She misses you though. She's been saying 'ma-ma-ma-ma' all day!" my mother teased as I listened to my lil baby girl repeat it. It made me smile through my tears.

"Okay mom. I'll be there in the morning to get her."

"Come in the afternoon because she got a playdate with Connie's granddaughter Sophia. We're taking them to the new indoor Play Palace!"

"Okay, well you guys have fun and take plenty of pics!" I urged before hanging up.

Before I could stuff it in the pocket of my dress, it rang. It was an unfamiliar number, but I answered it anyway.

"Don't hang up Tierra," Thaddeus pleaded. "I just wanted to apologize for all the dumb shit I've done lately. I was acting out of emotion and there's no excuse..."

"There sure ain't so bye..."

"Wait Tierra! I won't call you again. I just wanna tell you that I love you and Miracle, and I always will... I'm not gonna call you or harass you anymore. I'll just wait to hear from you. It's gonna be hard as hell, but I'm gonna give you the space and time you need."

What the hell was he talking about? No amount of time in the world was going to make me ever want to deal with his crazy ass ever again!

Not in a million years!

CHAPTER TWENTY-THREE

Thaddeus

Making that call to Tierra was the hardest call I ever had to make, but it was easier than telling her the results of the paternity test. As it turned out, Sheena's son Dillon was mine and I felt like shit for denying him when all he wanted was a father.

That day I picked up the documents from the clinic, I wanted to cry. To be honest, I really didn't know that little boy was mine, but I was so focused on being with Tierra that I didn't care if he was or not. At the time Sheena first approached me, I already had a family, so I didn't want another one. Can you believe that shit? I loved that woman and her baby girl so much that I was willing to throw away my own flesh and blood to be with Tierra. That shit was crazy, and I realize how wrong I was.

When I read those DNA results that said 99.9999% positive, I went from shock, to guilt, to happy that I had a kid of my own. Now it was up to me to step up and be a positive role model in Dillon's life.

"Who are you out there on the phone with Thaddeus?" Sheena yelled from the back door. "I need you to come in here and help me find a new school for Dillon that's close to here. Shit, Houston know they got too many fucking schools out here! Don't make no damn sense to have all these elementary schools!"

I rolled my eyes upward because my head had been pounding and banging ever since she up and moved herself into my place. She was pissed when she found out that I had swabbed Dillon behind her back, but obviously she had gotten over her anger. When I shared the results with her, less than five hours later she and Dillon were on my doorstep with everything she had brought with her when she moved here.

She just barged in my place and made herself comfortable. She had even taken everything out of my office and put it in the garage so she could make a room for Dillon. I didn't mind because he was my son and I wanted to provide for him, but she could've asked me first. It was like she had come in and was trying to take over my shit.

Trying not to overreact and cause a scene, I just took my ass inside and helped Sheena on the computer which was now in the den. Shaking my head at how much my life had changed in just a matter of a few days had me tripping. All I could do now was just go with the flow.

Soon as we were done enrolling Dillon into a charter school in our community, Sheena pulled me on the couch and told Dillon to go play with his trucks in his room. Without a fuss, our son ran off and did as he was told. I was impressed at how well-mannered he was.

"Babe, since you now know Dillon is yours and we're living together, you think we'll get married someday?" Sheena asked while we had some private time.

"Married? Where the hell did that come from?" I asked with a raised brow.

"From my heart silly!" she giggled as she snuggled up into my chest.

We had just gotten together as a family, and she was already trying to lock me down! Everything was happening just a little too fast for me. Of course, I wanted to help Sheena raise our son, but I was still very much in love with Tierra. That wasn't some shit that I could just turn off like a faucet because things had gotten a little bumpy. The kind of love I had for Tierra was strong enough to last for a lifetime, only I had to think and act smart after making a mess of things. Everything foul that I had done had only made things worse and pushed Tierra away. I hated myself for doing the shit!

I wasn't a woman beater. I had never laid my hands on any woman before in my life. But love made you do crazy things. Finding out that she had been fucking around on me hurt like hell. I mean, she had been cheated on by her husband, so why would she turn around and do the same thing to me? I didn't deserve that shit. I had been a good man to Tierra and a great father to Miracle. She should've taken that into consideration and treated me better.

"Babe, I'm talking to you. Why aren't you answering me?" Sheena pressed.

"Because you took me by surprise, that's why. To be honest Sheena, that thought ain't ever crossed my mind."

Shrugging my shoulders, I got up from the sofa and went over to the built-in bar to pour a drink. Sheena just had to say something slick.

"Am I stressing you out babe?"

"Honestly, yeah, a little."

"Well, I know how to help you relax," she wooed as she stood up and began tugging at the waistband of my gym shorts. They were easy access and it didn't take nothing but a second to whip that muthafucka out on demand. Sheena was asking for it.

Drawing me into the bedroom, Sheena softly closed the door and locked it behind her. "We have a good 20 minutes before Dillon starts knocking on that door. So how you want me baby?"

"On your knees," I stated boldly causing her to frown.

"I don't mind suckin' yo dick babe, but I need my shit licked sometimes too." She giggled as she came out of her clothes and began to undress me.

Fuck! The thought of putting my tongue in anyone else's pussy besides Tierra was messing up my mental. I needed another double shot before that happened.

"Why do you always have to get fucked up to make love to me?"

"Because it helps me relax Sheena. You gotta realize something... we're just getting to know each other all over again. Give me a chance to fall in love with you."

Yeah boy! A nigga had game like a muthafucka, but not enough to get out of eating Sheena's pussy! No, she wasn't letting me get away with that shit. She was so bold that she rolled me over onto my back and sat on my face! Tierra wasn't even that aggressive.

Rolling with it, I gripped onto Sheena's hips as I shoved my tongue in and out of her stash. The good smell and sweet taste made it easy for me to make love to her pussy with my mouth. Had her climaxing back to back.

Now my dick was hard, and I was ready to stick it in her oral canal because the one thing Sheena was great at was giving head. Had me shooting my kids down her throat within seconds and I was still good to go.

"Come here and let me give you what you've been begging me for." I whispered as I stroked the mixture of our juices up and down my erection.

Getting on her hands and knees, she tooted her ass upward to let me hit it from the back. This time I didn't want it like that. I needed to feel a warm body against mine.

"Nah, baby I'ma need you to ride me," I panted as I got on my back and gestured her right down onto my dick. "Damn ma' you tight as hell!"

The way her pussy was gripping my dick had me going. Oh and when a nigga closed his eyes and imagined that it was Tierra on top of me... I was busting immediately. I was about to call out Tierra's name until I opened my eyes and saw that it was Sheena sitting on top of me. Shit, good thing I did that. The last thing I'd want to do is call Sheena by the wrong name. I wasn't trying to fight the crazy broad.

"See, now that's how you're supposed to give it to me babe!" Sheena smiled as she cuddled up in my arms.

"Uh, are you gonna brush your teeth?" I asked.

"Damn babe! Can you just give me a minute to catch my breath?"

I didn't respond. As long as she didn't try to kiss me or breathe directly in my face, I guess I was good. It felt awkward cuddling with Sheena, but when Dillon came knocking at the door screaming for his mommy and daddy, it made it a little easier to accept. It was something I could even get used to.

"I'm coming Dillon!" she called out. "I'll go tend to our son while you get cleaned up," Sheena slipped out of bed and quickly made a dash for the bathroom. I heard her brushing her teeth, so I was happy about that. She emerged back into the bedroom and slid into her tank and shorts. "I was gonna cook dinner, but after you put it on me like that, I think I'll treat us at Cheesecake Factory tonight. It's Dillon's favorite."

As Sheena disappeared out of the room, I went and took a quick shower. While in there all I could do was try to figure out how I was engaged to Tierra just weeks ago and now Sheena and I were living together... and I had a son!

How the hell did this happen? I was supposed to be marrying Tierra and building a family with her!

Feeling lost in love, I tried my best to shake my thoughts of Tierra out of my head. I had to let it go, but the shit was hard to do!

Forcing a smile on my face, I went out in the den and interacted with my newly made family. It wasn't so bad though... it was just different. It was nothing like the life I had before. Especially how Tierra acted with me in public. I didn't know how truly ghetto she could be until we got to the restaurant and were stopped by two white girls before we made it inside.

Ignoring Sheena was even standing there the two high strung chicks rushed me and begged me to take a picture of them. I didn't see what was wrong with it, but Sheena... she made a big deal out of the whole thing.

"Don't you just see me standing here with my family? Your lil disrespectful asses gonna fly right by me and go to my man?" Sheena barked backing the two young chicks all the way up.

"Geesh!" the tall skinny one huffed. "We just wanted him to take a picture of us! It wasn't like we were trying to fuck him!"

"Oh, and you a bold bitch too... talking like that in front of our son!" Sheena said slyly as she reached around me and bopped the girl in the head with her handbag. That was enough to send both of them running to their car.

"Why you hit that lady like that mama?" Dillon looked up at Sheena and asked.

"Because she was being disrespectful to me and daddy. I can't let that happen baby. You'll understand when you get older," she reasoned like it wasn't a big deal that she had just done some shit that could get her ass locked up.

I sure wasn't ready for all that ghetto ass shit. Sheena was going to have to change up a few things if we were going to be together. As soon as we got seated, I started calling her on her flaws before ordering our drinks.

"Look Thaddeus, you're not in the position to tell me how to act. I'm a grown woman who just happens to be the mother of your only child... your son! So, the least you can do is let me be me," she huffed making yet another scene. I just shook my head and shut the fuck up. That was until she decided to enlighten me about one last thing. "In case you haven't noticed, I was doing a damn good job at it before we moved in with you!"

She rolled her eyes and smacked her lips as she sneered at the customers who were giving her funny looks. They were looking at her like she didn't belong in the restaurant in the bougie part of Houston. But she didn't give two shits about making a scene.

"Oh, and I have something to tell you too. I know you're gonna trip when you hear the news, but..."

"What is it now Sheena?" I asked scared to hear the answer.

"This morning I took a home pregnancy test and it came out positive. Now I know it's a little early and we have to get it confirmed by a doctor, but I'm pretty sure I'm pregnant babe! Isn't this great?!" Sheena shouted as tears began to flow. "You hear that Dillon? You're gonna be a big brother! Mommy and daddy are gonna have another baby!"

My stomach twisted in knots and I knew what Sheena was telling me could very well be true, but there was nothing I could do about it. It was my fault. I had been fucking her raw since she came back into my life.

"Are you happy?" Sheena pressed when she saw me down the drink that the waitress had just brought me.

With a hesitant nod, I ordered another double shot of Jack as I forced a smile. What else could I do?

That night, realizing that I was stuck in a relationship that I didn't pursue taught me a valuable lesson. Every choice that I made had a consequence. When you make bad decisions, you get even worse results.

I was tired of all the bad results and I was ready to turn my life around. If that meant spending the rest of my life with Sheena and the kids, so be it. I may have not asked for it, but I was definitely going to make the best of it.

Dammit! I guess shit between me and Tierra was really over!

CHAPTER TWENTY-FOUR

Jay

Sammy's funeral had us all drained. That was one of the longest days of my life, but what made it all better was when Tierra went to bed that night, she told me about the call she got from Thaddeus.

"I don't know why you even took that call babe. If you were still gonna speak to him, what was the purpose of the restraining order?" I asked.

I wasn't happy that she had spoken to that nigga, even if she did think that he wouldn't contact her anymore. That nigga was crazy if you asked me.

"I didn't know it was him that was calling me when I answered," she admitted.

"All the more reason why you shouldn't have answered. You have his number on blocked, so what'd you think he was gonna do to get in touch with you?"

"Jay please, it's been a long day baby. I don't wanna fight with you," she said with a weak frown.

"I'm sorry. I don't wanna fight with you either. I just don't want you being drawn back into his bullshit."

"I'm not... I promise you that I'm not."

"So, you really think he's gonna finally leave you alone?" I pressed as I stared at her while she changed into a short sexy silk gown.

As she tied her hair up, she looked down at me and smiled. "Yes, especially when I looked online after he called."

"What do you mean looked online? What was online?" I asked pulling her down onto the bed with me.

"That Sheena chick posted on his page that Thaddeus is her baby's daddy!" she laughed. "I have a feeling that's the real reason he backed off."

"That's good for him because at the rate he was going I thought I was gonna have to make his ass disappear," I blurted out without thinking. I was still holding on to that secret and I knew that made me no better than the next liar.

Thing was, I wasn't holding the secret from her because it would hurt her. Hell, if I had to do that shit all over again I would do it the exact same way! I had no regrets about getting rid of Dallas' crazy ass. The only reason I wasn't going to tell Tierra about what I had done was because I didn't want her to have to testify against me if the truth ever came out. I didn't need her involved. Dallas was gone and nobody missed him.

Maybe it wasn't fair to Miracle because technically that was the sperm donor who helped create her. That was okay though. I had enough love to give that beautiful little girl and her mother and it was enough to last a lifetime. I knew I could be a better father to Miracle than Dallas could have ever been.

"Why you get all quiet baby?" Tierra probed as she toyed in my facial hair.

"Just thinking..."

"About what?"

"About you, about me, about Miracle, shit about us as a family. How you feel about that baby?"

"About us?"

"Yeah, about us?"

"I don't know. I mean, this kinda came outta nowhere... so much has happened and..."

"I'm in love with you Tierra," I whispered looking her in the eyes. It didn't matter if she said it back or not. The way she gazed at me, made me feel her love.

"Awwww, I love you too baby!" Tierra cried and kissed me over and over.

"And you wanna be with me?"

"I thought we were together."

"I mean, sell your house, rent it out or whatever you have to do to let go of your past and start your future with me. You and Miracle can move in with me..."

"Are you sure you want a ready-made family?" she pressed with a serious expression.

"Shit, to be honest I'm tryna make this muthafucka bigger!" I laughed. "After being around Miracle and watching my sister go through losing a child, it made me appreciate life even more. Having kids is a beautiful blessing and I can't think of anyone else I'd rather share that with except you baby."

Laying all my cards on the table, I waited for Tierra to take the lead and boy did she. "So, how serious are you about us being together?"

"Dead ass serious!" I said frowning.

"Serious enough to make a commitment to me?"

"I'm already committed to you baby," I told her with a kiss to her lips. I knew what she was getting at, but I was way ahead of her. I had already got her a fat ass ring after I had to beat Thaddeus' down behind her. Once I did that shit, I knew she had to be mine in every way possible, with no room for another nigga to get the time of day from her.

"See, you always wanna play!" Tierra pouted playfully.

"I'm not playing. I just wasn't sure you wanted to get engaged again so soon after breaking it off with ol' boy," I admitted while trying to feel her out.

"I don't. I don't wanna get engaged."

Shit, what the fuck? Didn't she just say that she wanted me to commit to her? If she didn't wanna get engaged, what kind of commitment did she want from me?

"What?"

"I don't wanna get engaged baby... I wanna get married," she said shocking me.

"That's what you want huh?" I teased as I smiled at her. Then I rolled over and reached in the bottom drawer of the nightstand closest to my side of the bed. When I removed my hand, I brought out a black velvet drawstring bag containing a small box. "Well, I guess you don't want this then huh?"

"Stop playing with me Jay!" she screamed as she tussled with me to get the bag out of my hand. "What is that? Let me see! I do want it!"

"You don't even know what it is and you over here trying to kill me to get it!" I laughed and rolled out of the bed to stand up.

"Please Jay! Stop teasing me and show me what it is!"

"No, you said you didn't want it," I panted while dodging her grabs for the bag. She had me twisting and turning until we both landed on the floor. Then she got to tickling me. That did it! I let go of the bag.

Snatching it open, she saw the box and paused before handing it back to me. "No, you show me."

Noticing her hands trembling as she released the box, my heart melted. "Here baby," I said getting up from the floor to a kneeling position, so we were eye to eye. "Make me the happiest man in the world and marry me! We can run off to Vegas and do that shit tonight or we can plan a big ass wedding! Whatever you want, I'm down."

Tears cascaded down Tierra's flushed cheeks as I put the ring on her lockdown finger. Looking down at it, she began yelling as she tackled me back down to the floor. "Hell yeah! Hell yeah! I'll marry you on a boat with a goat eating green eggs and ham baby! I'll marry you anytime and anywhere you want to! Just make it soon!"

"What's the rush?" I asked.

"Well, remember when you just said that you wanted to make our family bigger..."

"Yeah."

"Well, you did just that baby!"

"Huh?" I repeated in confusion.

"Um, I'm sorta pregnant," Tierra replied softly with a shy expression on her face.

"You're what?"

"I'm pregnant!"

"Aw shit!" I yelled excitedly as I took her in my arms and kissed her.

Those words were like music to my ears and I couldn't wait to make love to my fiancée. *Y'all hear that shit? I said my FIANCÉE! And she was having my baby!*

Never had I been engaged in my life. Hell, I hadn't even truly been in love with a woman until I let myself fall for Tierra. I should've known from that first time we played hide and go get it when we were kids and I got to kiss her that I was going to be with her one day. I should've known...

"Come give me some of that good loving my husband to be!" Tierra urged as she sexily drew me on top of her.

Fulfilling all of her requests that night, I left her satisfied and sleeping peacefully on her side of the bed by eight. Still full of energy, I eased out of her hold and got my cell phone to look up some flights to Vegas. I was ready to take that big step.

Vegas here we come!!

EPILOGUE

Smooth

Three months later...

After Sammy's funeral, I kissed Tangi goodbye, packed up everything I had in the hotel, hopped in my truck and headed out. Seeing the tears flowing from Tangi's eyes after I bid her farewell almost made me change my mind, but I had to get away. No matter how much I loved her, this town held way too many painful memories for me to stay. I had decided to head to California. I had a cousin out there who lived in San Diego, and he said that I could come over there and stay with him for as long as I wanted to.

No matter how hard I tried not to, I kept reflecting back on watching my son's casket being lowered into the ground earlier. It shattered every piece of my heart. I was literally a broken man right now and there was nothing that could take that pain away. I had informed Jay of my decision and he had tried to talk me out of it. But once I told him how important it was for me to get away, he understood.

Now, here I was three short months later... *Who would've thought that I'd be returning to Houston so soon?*

KNOCK! KNOCK! KNOCK!

Standing on Tangi's doorstep, I waited for her to open the door. When she finally did, tears erupted from my eyes. She stood there smiling and crying as I reached for her. She hugged me tight as her body rocked with sobs. I knew that she was surprised to see me because we hadn't spoken the whole time that I was gone.

After several minutes, she released me and pulled me inside. "What are you doing here?" she asked as she wiped away her tears.

I looked at her swollen belly and touched it. I couldn't believe that she was pregnant again. "I came for you."

"How'd you know?"

"Your brother told me. I'm sorry that I didn't answer your calls. I just needed that time to myself, but when Jay called and told me that you were pregnant..."

"With twins!" she said with a huge smile on her face.

"What?" I asked as I stared at her in shock.

"I'm having twins!" she repeated.

"How far along are you?"

"Fifteen weeks, but as you can see, I'm already plump which was a concern for me. I thought something was wrong because of how fast my belly was growing, so I went to the doctor. She did an ultrasound the same day and…" She walked over to her purse and dug inside. She pulled out what looked like a little card and handed it to me.

Inside were ultrasound pictures that said 'Baby A' on one image and 'Baby B' on the other side. Tears sprang to my eyes as I stared at the images of my babies that were growing inside of Tangi's belly. It was like we were not only having a second chance at love, we were having a second chance at life! Two of them! I reached for Tangi and held her again.

"I love you Tangi. I never stopped loving you baby," I admitted as I nuzzled her neck.

"I love you too Sam."

Releasing her from my hold, I looked into her eyes. "Let's get married! Let's go down to city hall, get the marriage license and do the damn thing!"

"Really?" she asked.

"Really."

She nodded her head as we sealed the deal with a kiss. I fell in love with Tangi almost two years ago and I've been loving her ever since. We had faced some very tragic shit during that time, but we still were able to find our way back to each other.

I never thought I could be this happy again when Sammy died, but I am. I'm very happy to have my woman back in my life.

This time, I was never letting her go!

Tangi

When Smooth left, I was devastated. I couldn't believe that he would just leave me like that. We were both still grieving the loss of our baby boy, so I tried my best to be understanding. After trying to reach him the first two weeks after he left with no response, I just gave up and sank into a deep depression. I wasn't eating. I couldn't sleep. I just wanted to give up on life.

However, Tierra, my cousin Gina and Jay wouldn't let me do that. Even though I hadn't seen my cousin Gina in over three years, she was still more like a mom to me and Jay and had been ever since we were pretty much on our own as kids. I was fortunate enough to get her to stay and move in with me after the funeral so she could keep an eye on me. But then I still couldn't get out of this depressive state. She finally encouraged me to go to a support group. At first, I refused, but then she said she'd come with me. So, me, her and Tierra went to our first meeting. After a couple of weeks, I started feeling better.

Then I started getting nauseated and worn out. After a couple of weeks passed, Tierra encouraged me to go to the doctor. I was starting to get concerned because I had started gaining weight. When the doctor said that I was pregnant, I was floored. She could've knocked me over with a feather when she said that. I immediately called Sam, but he still wasn't taking my calls.

I didn't want to deliver the news in a text message, so I figured when he would decide to return my call, I'd tell him. So, imagine my surprise when he showed up on my doorstep. I couldn't believe that he was here. If I hadn't touched him, I would've thought that he was a figment of my imagination.

But he wasn't. He was here and he was holding me. And he wanted to marry me. I couldn't believe that after everything we had been through, he still loved me. God had taken me on a rollercoaster ride that I was sure was going to end with me being alone with about ten cats. But he didn't do me like that. As tears streamed from my eyes while I stared into the face of the man I loved, I sent the Lord a silent prayer of thanks.

Thanks for giving me my man back. Thanks for trusting me enough to bless me with two more babies. Thank you, God, for having my back. I won't let you down.

As Smooth and I took the reunion to the bedroom, I couldn't wait for him to get inside me. He always said he loved it when my kitty was pregnant, and it had been three long months since we had made love. I was anxious to get my clothes off.

I guess I was going to get that happy ending that nobody wanted me to have after all...

Tierra

Now that Tangi and Smooth were back together, my man and I could finally tie the knot. As much as Jay and I wanted to become husband and wife, we couldn't do it without our best friends by our sides. Tangi was in such an awful state that I wouldn't dare do this without her. I needed Tangi there with me. When I found out she was pregnant, I was ecstatic because we were going to go through our pregnancies together.

However, I still had something she longed to have... her baby's father by her side. Jay had spoken to Smooth a couple of times, informing him about Tangi's pregnancy, but he hadn't found his way back home until yesterday. Thank God!

Tangi didn't deserve to go through that pregnancy without him, especially since she was expecting twins. It was funny how life worked out. I was 21 weeks pregnant with my second child and Tangi was 15 weeks, but she was bigger than I was. At least we were doing it together. We had the same doctor, were registered at the same hospital and let's not talk about the shopping trips we were going to have.

I was so happy to be sharing this time with her. So, here we were now... she and Smooth were engaged again and planning their wedding at the courthouse. But, Jay and I were flying out to Vegas next weekend along with our best friends and close family. I couldn't wait to become Jay's wife. Even though Tangi was my best friend, so was her brother. I couldn't have asked God for a better man for myself and father to my daughter.

Miracle was thriving and flourishing as a toddler and I couldn't be happier. She was such a joy in my life, my greatest gift. Jay had stepped in as her daddy and he really was a great father. I hated that Thaddeus was involved from the beginning, only because I never wanted to confuse my baby about who her father was. She wasn't old enough to know that Dallas was her real father or that he was dead. I do have plans to tell her about him when she's older though... but for now, she's going to have to get used to Jay being her dad because after the way Thaddeus behaved, he would never see my child again.

With all the child killings going on in the world these days, I'd be damn if I'd ever put my baby girl in harm's way like that. Thaddeus had stayed out of my way since our last conversation. I saw that Sheena was pregnant again, so I guess she was keeping him busy. Thank God.

I needed her to keep his ass as far away from me as possible.

I hope I'm carrying a little boy because then I'd have my pair. I knew how much Jay wanted a son and I wanted to give him that. After all, he gave me my happily ever after...

Jay

When Smooth told me that he had made the decision to come back home, I was glad to hear it. There was no way my sister should be going through this pregnancy by herself. She already had to grieve without him, so even if I had to go over there and drag him back home, I was just gonna have to do what I had to do. Tangi didn't deserve all the shit that had happened to her over the past year. She wasn't a bad person... she had just made some really bad choices. But the important thing was that she learned from her mistakes and knew better now.

Not to say that she didn't know any better before, but she was in a better mind frame now. I don't know what made her fuck with Dallas and risk her friendship with Tierra. I was glad that nigga was gone though. I had no regrets about getting rid of him because he was causing problems for the two women I loved most in the world, besides my mom of course.

I had always been protective of my sister ever since we were younger. That was never going to stop. That's why when I had made arrangements for me and Tierra to get married and Tangi's condition was getting worse, I canceled the plans without hesitation. Family came first, always. There was no way I was going to run off to Vegas to get married when my little sister was falling apart. The great thing about it was that Tierra understood and agreed with me one hundred percent. I was glad too because there was no way I could do this shit with those two women by myself. Hell no!

Damn! I truly have a real one with Tierra. After all my sister had put her through, Tierra cared about me and my family, just like I cared about her and Miracle. She even had me calling Smooth like crazy when Tangi popped up pregnant.

That nigga was happy as all outdoors and brought his ass right back home where he belonged. Now he and Tangi were in a better place. It seemed as if we were all in a better place.

Tangi and Tierra's friendship was back on track and even more solid than before. Tangi and Smooth had their relationship back and it was stronger than ever. And as for me and Tierra... well, we were tighter than any two people could be. I loved that woman more than anything in the world.

She was stuck with me now...

Thaddeus

I rolled my eyes as Sheena continued to give me reasons why we should get married. I was so tired of going through this shit with her. It almost made me want to run off and marry her today just to shut her up. But I didn't want to do that if I wasn't ready. I was still in love with Tierra and I didn't know when I'd shake those feelings off. It was hard when Sheena was constantly acting ghetto and embarrassing me, everywhere we went.

Perfect example: Sheena and I were in the Target store shopping for baby stuff. You would think that she'd be happy about that, but she wasn't. She was complaining about us having two kids out of wedlock.

"Don't you think I deserve to be your wife now that we're having our second child?" she asked.

"I told you already that this isn't the time or place for this discussion," I said.

"Then when is the time?"

"When we get home."

Suddenly, she was squinting her eyes. I wondered what that was about. "What's wrong with you?" I asked.

"Ain't that your ex over there?" she asked as she nodded her head in a direction behind me.

I couldn't turn my head fast enough to see who she was talking about. Sure enough, there was Tierra and that Jay nigga looking at baby furniture. Why was she looking for baby furniture when Miracle's nursery was completely furnished? As she moved in the opposite direction, I noticed not only her swollen belly, but the huge ring on her finger.

"If you don't stop staring!" Sheena said from behind me as she bopped me upside the head with her purse.

"Ouch, shit!" I fumed as I turned in her direction. "What the fuck you do that for?"

"Because you seemed to have forgotten that I was standing right here!"

"I wish I could forget that easy," I mumbled under my breath.

"What'd you say, huh? Huh? What you said?"

"Sssshhh! You gon' make them look this way and shit!"

"HA! Too late! They already looking at you like you smell like shit!" she laughed.

I slowly turned and Tierra and Jay were staring at me with disgust on their faces. Once we made eye contact, they turned on their heels and headed in the direction of the exit. Damn! I was gonna go over there and say hello. Sheena was always doing some shit with her ol' loud mouth ass!

"You do know she doesn't want you right?" Sheena asked loudly so everyone in the whole damn store could hear her.

"Let's go!" I said as I grabbed her hand and pulled her toward the exit.

"Where are we going? I thought we were gonna get some stuff that we needed for the baby!"

"We can do that another time. Right now, I just wanna get the hell up outta here!"

"I hope you ain't finna go chase behind that damn woman who don't want you. I mean, she's clearly moved on!" Sheena laughed.

I didn't bother answering. I just got in the truck and prayed that I'd be able to deal with this woman for the rest of my life. When we pulled into the parking lot of the courthouse, she turned to look at me.

"What are we doing here?"

"You wanted to get married right?"

"Yea, but..."

"But what? Let's just do it and get it over with before I change my mind."

"Wow! No proposal or nothing romantic?"

"Nah, we ain't got time for that. You wanna get married or not?"

"Yea!"

"Then let's go!"

We hopped out the truck and I prayed that I was doing the right thing. I was going to make sure that I was a constant figure for my kids even if that meant tying myself down to their mother. What other option did I have? I mean, Tierra had moved on so there was no chance for us to get back together. I may as well make the best of my own life.

God please don't let this be a mistake...

The end!!

Withdrawn

CPSIA information can be obtained
at www.ICGtesting.com
Printed in the USA
LVHW111134290919
632606LV00002B/272/P